Feral

Feral

SHERI WHITEFEATHER

HEAT | NEW YORK

THE BERKLEY PUBLISHING GROUP
Published by the Penguin Group
Penguin Group (USA) Inc.
375 Hudson Street, New York, New York 10014, USA
Penguin Group (Canada), 90 Eglinton Avenue East, Suite 700, Toronto, Ontario M4P 2Y3, Canada
(a division of Pearson Penguin Canada Inc.)
Penguin Books Ltd., 80 Strand, London WC2R 0RL, England
Penguin Group Ireland, 25 St. Stephen's Green, Dublin 2, Ireland (a division of Penguin Books Ltd.)
Penguin Group (Australia), 250 Camberwell Road, Camberwell, Victoria 3124, Australia
(a division of Pearson Australia Group Pty. Ltd.)
Penguin Books India Pvt. Ltd., 11 Community Centre, Panchsheel Park, New Delhi—110 017, India
Penguin Group (NZ), 67 Apollo Drive, Rosedale, Auckland 0632, New Zealand
(a division of Pearson New Zealand Ltd.)
Penguin Books (South Africa) (Pty.) Ltd., 24 Sturdee Avenue, Rosebank, Johannesburg 2196, South Africa

Penguin Books Ltd., Registered Offices: 80 Strand, London WC2R 0RL, England

This book is an original publication of The Berkley Publishing Group.

This is a work of fiction. Names, characters, places, and incidents either are the product of the author's imagination or are used fictitiously, and any resemblance to actual persons, living or dead, business establishments, events, or locales is entirely coincidental. The publisher does not have any control over and does not assume any responsibility for author or third-party websites or their content.

PRINTING HISTORY
Heat trade paperback edition / December 2011

Library of Congress Cataloging-in-Publication Data

Whitefeather, Sheri.
   Feral / Sheri Whitefeather. — Heat trade paperback ed.
     p. cm.
   ISBN 978-0-425-24332-9
   1. Shapeshifting—Fiction. I. Title.
   PS3623.H5798F47 2011
   813'.6—dc23

                                        2011028164

PRINTED IN THE UNITED STATES OF AMERICA

10 9 8 7 6 5 4 3 2 1

Prologue

Lareina stood in the shadows, churning with hunger.

She had been stalking him, watching him—this one called Noah. She'd heard that his people possessed some sort of special magic, or "medicine," as they called it, and she hoped that this would keep him alive after she was finished with him. Not for his sake, but for hers.

She moved forward, and as she did, her dress swished around her ankles. She was naked beneath the embroidered fabric, and she knew that she was beautiful. In her human form men desired her, yet none had lived to tell of her charms. She needed someone to survive, to become the creature she was.

She headed for the cantina, where Noah was spending his evening.

Barreling through the door, she held her head high. Women were prohibited from entering drinking establishments in this area. But Lareina didn't care if anyone tried to stop her.

The cantina wasn't crowded. Only a handful of men gathered at the bar. They all turned to gape at her, including Noah. She returned his gaze. She smiled at him, too, her lips curving ever so slightly.

The proprietor, a thick-bodied man with his stomach hanging over his pants, waved his arms at her.

"No whores!" he said.

She stared straight at him. "I am not a whore."

He looked her up and down. "You are not a lady, either."

That produced a round of chuckles from the patrons. Annoyed by their male foolishness, she returned her attention to Noah. He wasn't laughing.

The proprietor bellowed at him, "Get your slut out of here."

"She doesn't belong to me," Noah responded, without taking his gaze from Lareina's.

No one believed him. But why would they? Especially now that she was striding toward him.

She stood next to him. He smelled of soap, salt, and tequila, the combination strangely stirring.

"Who are you?" he asked, as the others watched.

She didn't give her identity away. Instead, she touched the side of his face. He was young and handsome, with strong features, deep-set eyes, and shiny hair falling bluntly to his shoulders.

"Out!" the fatty man snapped again.

She wanted to growl at the intrusion, but she couldn't. Maybe later she would come back to kill him. Or maybe later it wouldn't matter. Her priority was Noah.

Since the trap had already been set, she turned and walked away, exiting the cantina. She waited a moment, her immortal heart thumping.

Footsteps sounded behind her.

She proceeded toward the woods, aware that Noah followed, his now-familiar scent swirling in the breeze.

Once she was safe within the trees, she stopped and turned. He approached her, and she beckoned him, peeling off her dress and tossing it aside.

He pulled open his shirt and undid his pants. Apparently he no longer cared who she was. He didn't say a word and neither did she.

Anxious, he grabbed her, and they tumbled to the ground, crushing leaves in their lustful wake.

He freed his erect penis and plunged into her. She smiled like the seductress she was. He was deliciously carnal, but he was no match for her. She thrust back against him, creating a brutal rhythm.

His breaths rasped against her ear, and she rolled her tongue along the cords in his neck and down the front of his chest, where his shirt spilled open.

He groped her flanks and hammered her into the earth. Dirt stuck to her bared flesh, twigs jabbing her backside.

She flipped their bodies until she was on top, riding him, her legs taut around him. In his excitement, he roamed his hands over her, fondling her breasts, pinching her nipples, pushing a finger into her navel.

She kept moving, creating friction. He groaned his pleasure, and she relished the feeling.

Eager for more, she bit at his lips, drawing specks of blood and making herself climax. Heat ripped through her veins just as Noah shuddered and his seed burst from his loins.

Relentless, she bit at his lips again, only now her fangs pushed through her gums with knifelike precision. Her nails turned to claws, and her muscles elongated, her body getting bulkier, stronger.

Transforming until the animal emerged.

Moonlight shimmered through the branches, manifesting a soft light and allowing her prey the opportunity to witness what was happening to him.

Fear flashed across his handsome face, distorting his already bloodied mouth.

Lareina ripped into him, shredding his flesh. Ribbons of red streamed down his virile young body. He attempted to fight her off, but she intensified the attack.

On and on it went.

Harder. Deeper.

More fang. More claw. More sweet, crimson blood.

She growled with the power that possessed her, and finally, finally, she released him.

Barely breathing, he slipped into unconsciousness.

She peered curiously at him, batting him one last time with her paw. She couldn't come back and tend to his wounds. She could do nothing to help save him.

Still in cat form, she ran through the woods toward the hills, leaving him at his own mutilated mercy.

One

PRESENT DAY, SANTA CLARITA VALLEY, CALIFORNIA

The safari-themed fund-raiser presented khaki-colored table-cloths and centerpieces with flowers that grew wild on the property. Lights twinkled in the trees, and cutouts of lions, leopards, and tigers mimicked animals that lived there.

Jenny had hosted plenty of outdoor dinners before, but tonight she was nervous.

She stood off to the side, scanning the guests. Earlier in the day, she'd received a generous donation, and the anonymous donor had claimed that he or she would be attending the fund-raiser this evening and providing another substantial sum.

Enough to literally save this place.

Her heart hadn't quit pounding since she'd gotten the news. Would the donor actually come through? God, she hoped so. Big Cat Canyon, the exotic feline rescue her grandfather had founded, was her lifeblood, and she was on the verge of losing it.

"Any idea who it is?" Matt asked from beside her.

She turned toward him. With his golden blond hair and noticeable blue eyes, the family resemblance was clear. He was her cousin, but he looked like he could be her brother, maybe even her twin, though they were a few years apart.

"No," she said. "Do you?"

"No, but wouldn't it be funny if it's a guy who has designs on you?"

"What makes you say that?"

"Because rich men are notorious for using money to get a woman's attention. Stuff like that happens all the time."

She shot him a get-real glance. "The donation isn't about me. It's about the rescue."

"Really, cuz. I could have stumbled onto something here. The donor is being all cryptic and dramatic for a reason, and the reason could be in his pants. What if he's setting you up to be his mistress?"

She refused to entertain the theory. "That's ridiculous." Jenny was a zoologist who, most of the time, ran around in dirt-smudged jeans and no makeup. "I'm not the mistress type. I don't wear glamorous dresses and go to parties." These fund-raisers were as fancy as she got, and even now she was simply attired in a crisp blouse, a knee-length skirt, and flat boots, with her wavy hair clipped into a tidy ponytail.

"So maybe he wants to spruce you up. Or maybe he's into natural girls. Maybe he thinks a chick who rescues exotic cats is sexy. He might even be someone you already know."

The anonymous donation didn't make sense coming from someone she already knew. None of her members or supporters had ever donated *that* kind of money before. The downturn in the economy was playing havoc with their checkbooks. Their offerings were getting smaller, not bigger.

"Was it an online donation?" Matt asked.

"No. It was a check. But it was issued from an accounting firm. A big fancy place in LA. I looked them up online."

"Whose signature was on the check?"

"I don't know. It wasn't legible."

Once again, she scanned the guests. There were almost a hundred people there, and some had already finished their meals and wandered into the silent-auction tent, checking out the items on display.

"Whoever the donor is, he or she is a stranger," she said.

"Okay, but I still think it could be a guy who has designs on you, especially with that kind of money involved. Oh, wow. What if it's him?"

"Him who?"

Matt gestured with his chin. "The dude at the second table, sitting next to the woman in the bedazzled top."

She shifted her gaze to the aforementioned people. The man in question was as ancient as a moldy hill, and the sparkly old lady was probably his wife. "Knock it off."

Matt grinned at his little joke.

She blew out a sigh, and he laughed. She wished that he would take something seriously just once. Her cousin was twenty-six going on twelve. He'd been weaned on the rescue, too, but he preferred the sand and surf. He lived in a messy apartment in Santa Barbara with a zillion other skater/surfers. He visited her and the cats only when the mood struck him.

"Holy shit," he said suddenly. "I found him. This time for sure."

She refused to follow his line of sight. "Just quit, okay? Stop it."

"No, really, Jenny. I was just kidding around before, but I'm serious now. Take a gander at the guy coming out of the auction tent."

Like an idiot, she glanced in that direction. Then she did what she'd been taught not to do. She stared.

Moving with the rangy grace of one of her cats, he was tall and leanly muscled, with bronzed skin and long, licorice-black hair. While the wind snapped at his clothes, autumn-tinged leaves fluttered in dust-devilish circles around his feet, as if the environment, the place she called home, were attaching itself to him with magnetic force.

"You'd better be careful," Matt said. "A guy like that will fuck you raw."

Jenny gulped the night air, blasting her lungs with a much-needed breath. "No one is going to do anything to me."

"Oh, yeah? Well, he's coming this way, and if he's the man with the money, you're in trouble."

It was pointless to ask Matt to stick around. He was already searching for an escape route. Clearly, he didn't want to get involved other than to dole out unsolicited advice.

He gestured to the buffet line. "I'm going to grab some chow."

"Go ahead." She wasn't going to let him fill her head with nonsense. The hunk of burning man walking in her direction wasn't going to save this place for a piece of tail, least of all, hers.

She didn't move forward. She waited for the stranger to approach her. When he did, she plastered a smile on her face and hoped it wasn't wobbling.

"Jenny Lincoln?" he asked.

"Yes."

"I'm Noah. My accountant sent a check over today."

Oh, Lord. He *was* the donor, and up close he was even more handsome, with a wildly ethnic edge: deep, piercing eyes and cheekbones chiseled to perfection.

Before she lost her manners, she extended her hand. "Thank you. It was an incredibly generous donation."

His hand enveloped hers, and a jolt of heat, of sheer sexual energy, nearly knocked her off of her feet. She actually planted her boots in the ground to keep herself steady.

"There's more where that came from," he said.

The heat? she wondered.

He continued, "But I'm not going to give it to you tonight."

She blinked out of her haze. He was referring to the rest of the money.

"I'd like to meet with you privately," he said. "And I want you to give me a tour of the rescue."

She caught her breath. That was doable. "I'd be glad to show you around." Why wouldn't he want to see the facility he was sponsoring before he handed over another check? That made total sense.

He suggested the when and where. "Tomorrow morning around nine? At the main gate?"

"I'll clear my schedule for you."

He fixed his dark gaze on her. "Good."

Suddenly she realized that he hadn't told her his last name. She couldn't Google him later and find out more about him. But she assumed he didn't want her to have that advantage.

He smiled, but it didn't soften the moment. It actually made him seem more predatory.

"I'll see you tomorrow," he said.

"Yes, I'll see you," she parroted.

He didn't move, so she waited for him to walk away. Instinct told her not to turn her back on him.

Instinct?

Was she making too much of this? Feral as he seemed, he wasn't one of her cats.

But still, she waited.

He finally departed, walking away with the same feline grace with which he'd appeared, light on his feet, his muscles bunching and rolling.

As he disappeared into the crowd, she put her hand against her heart, struggling to calm the erratic beats. Matt was right. She needed to be careful of the man with the money.

In the morning, Noah returned to Big Cat Canyon. He parked his truck, climbed out of it, and activated the car alarm. He owned other vehicles, but the four-wheel-drive Ford fit his mood and the terrain.

He headed toward the front entrance and saw Jenny in the distance. He'd expected her to be on time. He suspected that she'd been early. He'd sensed her nervousness last night, and it was running rampant today, too.

He closed the gap and approached the gate. They looked at each other through the bars, as if there were a cage between them.

Noah said, "Hello."

She responded with a shaky, "Hi," and unlocked the gate.

Her wariness aroused him. Everything about her gave him a rush. He'd been preparing to take her as his lover.

Take being the key word.

He lowered his chin and studied her, making his perusal

obvious. She was fresh-scrubbed and free of cosmetics. Tendrils of wavy blond hair fought to escape a girlish ponytail. He was dying to see her hair loose, to run his hands through it, to tug on it with masculine vigor.

She glanced away, but he kept looking at her, enjoying the chase.

"Tell me about this place," he said, prodding her to engage with him. "Give me the sales pitch."

Her gaze found his, even if her voice wasn't quite steady. "It's not a sales pitch. It's home for captive-bred animals that have nowhere else to go."

Nervous as she was, her dedication shined through. That made her all the more fascinating.

She continued by saying, "My grandfather was a large-animal veterinarian, and this used to be his ranch. When he retired, he turned it into an exotic cat rescue."

Noah already knew a bit of the background based on what he'd read on the Big Cat Canyon website, but he was curious to know more, especially with her relaying the details.

He asked, "What motivated him to do that?"

"He volunteered his services at other rescues, and he realized how grave the need was for more facilities like this. We have an on-site medical-care center that enables us to perform examinations and surgeries without transporting the cats. We provide exercise trails for the animals, too." She waited a beat. "For our guests, we have picnic areas. We also have a gift shop."

Coffee mugs and plush toys didn't interest him. Nonetheless, he was ready to start the tour.

It began with the food preparation area, which was impressively spotless, with several employees already hard at work.

Jenny said, "We prepare nutritionally balanced meat-based diets. They're flash frozen with no by-products, hormones, antibiotics, or preservatives." She added, "Felids are strict carnivores."

Noah remained deliberately quiet, allowing her to educate him about something he knew far too well. He was part "felid" and he was carnivorous as hell.

She went on to say, "A felid is a member of the *felidae* family, which is the biological family of cats, and felids belong to two subfamilies: *pantherinae* and *felinae*."

Once again he stayed silent. She'd yet to relax in his presence, and he reveled in the anxious sound of her breathing and the pulse that beat quickly at her neck.

"Sorry." She made a face. "Sometimes I get carried away. Those words are probably just mumbo jumbo to you."

"No, it's interesting." He pushed the boundaries of who he was, playing his predatory game. "I'm curious—what are the scientific terms associated with mountain lions?"

"They belong to the *felinae* subfamily. Their genus and species name is *Puma concolor*, but it used to be *Felis concolor*."

Noah considered himself a subspecies. A hybrid, for lack of a better description.

She tilted her pretty little head. "Are mountain lions your favorite exotic cat?"

As if he had a choice. "Yes."

She continued the lesson. "Aside from the scientific terms, they have a slew of other names. The *Guinness Book of World Records* recognizes them as the animal with the most names. The most common is cougar, of course."

"And here I thought a cougar was an older woman who dated younger men."

She wrinkled her nose, and they both laughed. Apparently she didn't like the urban slang definition any better than he did.

A moment later, she said, "Some of the other names are puma, catamount, mountain screamer, painter, mountain demon, mountain devil, ghost cat, sneak cat, Florida Panther, Indian devil—"

"Like me?" He made another deliberately bad joke, but it wasn't intended to be funny and neither of them laughed. "I'm from the Seminole Nation."

She studied him. "So you're Native American?"

"Yes, but I lived in Mexico for quite a while. I'm fluent in Spanish. I speak the Mvskoke language, too. But it's been a long time since I used it." He didn't fit into modern Seminole society. He didn't fit anywhere, except for the environment he'd created for himself. "I descend from the Tiger Clan."

"Oh." She made a perplexed expression. "But you're more interested in mountain lions?"

"In the old days the Seminole referred to mountain lions as 'tigers.'"

"I knew that European explorers mistook them for tigers, but I wasn't aware of Seminole history." She offered to oblige him. "Would you like to head over to see the mountains lions now? We have two that live here."

"I'd rather see the other cats first." Noah wanted to save the most important for last.

The tour continued with an introduction to a four-hundred-pound Bengal tiger. She was obviously still thinking about his association to the Tiger Clan, even if he wasn't connected to the animal in a literal sense.

They stood on the other side of the tiger's compound and watched it sleep.

"His name is Ankal," Jenny said. "It means 'whole' in Hindu. We chose that for him because when we rescued him he was broken, physically and emotionally, and we strived to make him whole. He came from an abusive situation."

Noah gazed at the napping tiger. He seemed content, or as content as a captive-bred creature could be.

"When he first arrived, he used to hide in his den when the keepers approached his enclosure. Now he plays in his pool when they're around, splashing and showing off."

Ankal yawned as if he was bored by the conversation. Noah quirked a smile. Jenny did, too.

She remarked, "In the wild, tigers hunt between dusk and

dawn and consume between thirty to ninety pounds of food at one sitting."

"How do they make a kill?" He intended to ask her the same question about mountain lions when the time came, even if he knew as much as or more about them than she did. But that was part of the thrill, of what had led him to her.

She responded, "Tigers stalk, chase, and attack, then bring down their prey with a bite to the nape of the neck or the throat. They're considered man-eaters, too. They'll consume human flesh."

"Ankal isn't as timid as he looks."

"None of them are."

Noah knew that better than anyone.

She interrupted the quiet. "Ankal's best friend is an African lion named Larry. They explore the trails together."

"Larry the lion?"

She laughed a little. "They don't all have exotic names."

He considered the lion and tiger's alliance. "They wouldn't get along in the wild, would they?"

"No. But it's different when they're in captivity."

He got curious about her social life. "What about you? Who's your best friend?"

She tucked a stray piece from her ponytail behind her ear, struggling, it seemed, to answer. Then she admitted, "I don't have one. I've always been more of a loner."

So was he. But that was indicative of the subspecies he'd been turned into. There had been a time when he'd enjoyed sharing his life with other people, when he'd felt a gentle connection to humanity. But those feelings were long gone.

Without further discussion, they proceeded on the tour, where more tigers were contained. They visited Larry the lion, too. After that, they stopped to admire two spotted leopards.

"They belonged to a Las Vegas entertainer who struggled to give them up," she said. "He treated them well and loved them. But he couldn't make ends meet."

"Much in the way you're having trouble keeping this place going?"

Her blue eyes locked onto his. "Your generosity is making a difference."

"I haven't given you the rest of the donation yet."

"I was talking about what you already provided."

"That's not enough to keep you out of the red."

"The second half will be."

"There are going to be strings attached, Jenny."

Her breath rushed out. "What type of strings?"

He suspected that she already knew it would be sexual, but he wasn't ready to divulge the details. "We'll talk about it later. Now, tell me about leopards. What's unique about the manner in which they hunt?"

She cleared her throat. "Sometimes they drag their kill into trees and hang them there. They're the only big cat that does that."

Fascinated by the ever-thudding pulse at her neck, he moved

closer to her. Instantly her body temperature rose. He could feel the heat.

"They're magnificent," he said about the leopards, but he could have been saying it about her, too.

"People often mix them up with jaguars and cheetahs. But the cheetah is leaner and swifter, actually the fastest animal on land, with solids spots and tear marks running from its eyes to its mouth. And the jaguar—"

"Is a car," he interjected.

She blinked, looking every bit the nervous scientist she was.

He smirked. "Sorry; couldn't help myself."

"No, it's okay. I was prattling."

"And I have an XK convertible."

"Is that a Jaguar?"

He nodded. "I'll let you drive it sometime."

"I don't think I'd be good at driving something like that."

"It doesn't take any special skill."

She fussed with the loose strands of her hair, as she'd done earlier, trying to tuck them back into her ponytail. She changed the subject, too, returning to chatter mode. "Are you ready to meet the small cats? We have a bobcat and three African servals. Mountain lions are considered small cats, too, even if they're the same size as some of the big cats."

"Really?" He acted surprised.

"The major difference between small cats and big cats is the hyoid bone that connects the tongue to the roof of their mouth. In big cats it produces the ability to roar, but in smaller cats it doesn't. Mountain lions can't roar. But they can purr, like other small cats."

Noah could purr. He could do it with the best of them.

Jenny took him to see the bobcat and the servals, and an affectionate female serval came up to the enclosure, eager for attention.

"That's Cookie," Jenny said. "She's as sweet as her name."

Typical of her breed, the cat resembled a cheetah, but smaller and with big pointed ears. "How did you acquire her?"

"Her owner died and left her orphaned."

Noah had outlived his family, too, but after a century of being alone, he'd learned to suppress his memories.

"Let's go," he said, letting her know he wanted to see the mountain lions.

She took him down a winding path that led to their enclosures, and the sun zigzagged through the trees. But regardless of how good daylight felt upon his skin, he still felt cold inside.

As he'd suspected, the mountain lions took an alert and territorial interest in him. Housed separately, they watched him through keen eyes.

Then one of them let out a low growl.

In the midst of the tension, Jenny glanced at Noah, seemingly aware of his catlike body language. No doubt she'd noticed his mannerisms from the start, only now they were more pronounced. He wasn't able to help it.

"That's Valiente," she said, a bit uncomfortably.

"Valiant" in Spanish. "What's his background?"

"He came from a roadside zoo. He lived in a crate that was barely big enough for him to turn around in. He's fearful of wide-open spaces because all he knew was being locked up in a small area. He won't roam his full enclosure, but we're hoping that someday he will."

"How long has he been here?"

"About a year. He's our newest member." She motioned to the other one. "And this is our oldest resident, the first cat my grandfather saved. His name is Sandy. I chose it for him when I was a child."

Noah merely nodded. Mountains lions varied in hues, but most people would describe them as tan, beige, or sandy. The name fit, especially coming from a child.

"They're solitary animals," she said. "Elusive. Males and females get together to mate, but that only lasts for a few days. Other than that, they avoid each other." A slight pause, then, "I mentioned earlier that they can purr, but their vocabulary also includes whistles, chirps, and hisses."

As if for effect, Valiente growled again.

She talked on. "They're most known for their nails-on-a-chalkboard-type scream. That's where the 'mountain screamer' name comes from. Females screech that way to let male lions know when they're sexually receptive."

She glanced away, and he suspected that she'd never been

uncomfortable saying "sexually receptive" in that context before. The scientist in her was faltering.

He smiled to himself. "What are their hunting practices like?"

"They're ambush predators. They stalk their prey from hidden areas, then jump out and inflict a suffocating bite to the neck. With larger prey, they eat the heart and liver first and save the carcass for another meal."

He roamed his gaze over her. "Can you imagine having something eat your heart right out of your chest?"

Her voice vibrated. "I'd prefer not to imagine it."

Aroused by her vulnerability, he said, "I want you to come to my place of business tomorrow night."

"What type of business is it?"

"A private sex club."

Speechless, she all but stared at him.

He ignored her reaction.

She finally spoke. "I'm not going to have sex with a bunch of strangers. I'd never do that, not even to save the rescue."

"I have no intention of sharing you with anyone. My interest in you is personal. Intimate," he added softly.

She didn't respond, but she shivered a little, making him want her that much more.

He continued, "All that's required of you tomorrow night is to come to the club. That's all you have to do for the rest of the donation."

"You're not going to expect me to sleep with you?"

"No. But eventually I want you to be my lover."

"What if I never want to be with you?"

"Then it won't happen."

"But you're going to try to seduce me so it does?"

He was already seducing her. "There's no harm in me trying, is there?"

She went silent again. Then she asked, "What sorts of activities go on at this club of yours?"

"Come there tomorrow night and find out."

"I want to know ahead of time. I want to know what to expect."

"Where's the adventure in that?"

"You're not being fair."

No, he wasn't. He was being an ambush predator, much like the mountain lions she'd just told him about. But since he was part lion, he was a natural ambusher. He couldn't help it any more than a wild cat could. "If you want the rest of the donation, then come to the club. It's as simple as that."

"This is an indecent proposal."

He shrugged. He was what he was. "I'll send a town car for you. The driver will pick you up at nine, and you should arrive at the club around ten." He roamed his gaze over her. "Wear something provocative."

She frowned. "I don't have those sorts of clothes in my wardrobe."

Of course she didn't. But that was part of what attracted him to her. He removed his wallet and extended a wad of cash. "Buy whatever you need."

She took a step back. "I—"

He nudged the money toward her again. "Just do it. Enjoy making yourself pretty for me."

"This is out of my realm. Men like you are out of my realm."

And women like her were out of his. But he was tired of the girls from the club. He hungered for a more challenging prey, and Jenny was exactly what he'd been hoping for.

He baited her. "I'm not going to stand here and argue with you about it. Either come to the club or not. Take my offer or leave it."

She took it; she agreed to the terms of his *indecent* proposal, but she looked as pale as the moon on the night he'd been attacked all those years ago. Still, he knew that she wouldn't back out.

Jenny was in for the kill.

Two

The following afternoon, Jenny belabored her decision. Could she do this? Could she actually do it?

She weighed her odds for the umpteenth time that day. If she didn't get the rest of the donation, she stood to lose the rescue. The place Grandpa had built and the place she'd strived to maintain might be forced to close its doors.

She'd become a zoologist to further her education and benefit Big Cat Canyon. She grew up on the rescue. It was her heart. Her soul. Her everything.

One night at Noah's club. One night and her financial struggle would end. With the money he was offering, the animals in her care would continue to have a safe and loving home. So, yes, she was absolutely, positively going to do this. She was going to get that damned donation from him and keep her rescue.

Determined to follow through, she called Matt and asked him to help her prepare for the evening. What she'd told Noah about not having a best friend was true. She didn't have anyone except Matt to confide in, and she involved him only because he'd already predicted that something like this was going to happen.

Well, not exactly like this. Not the sex club angle.

Hours later, Matt accompanied her to the mall in search of an outfit, and the end result was a short, shimmery white dress with a low-cut neckline. She'd bought some delicate lingerie to go with it because her usual underwear would have fit poorly beneath it. Her shoes were flesh-colored pumps, and her evening bag complemented the shoes and dress, or so she'd been told. She'd relied on the salesgirl's opinion to help her put it all together.

Since she didn't have a clue how to do her hair or makeup, she'd gone to a fancy salon and let them work their supposed magic.

Noah had told her to enjoy making herself pretty for him, but she wasn't having the least bit of fun. In fact, as she stood in front of the mirror in her room, she felt ridiculous.

Her hair was a mass of blond fluff, way too big and way too full. Her pink lips and smoky eyes looked weird, too.

Matt knocked on her bedroom door and called out, "Are you ready yet?"

She called back, "Yes, you can come in."

He entered the room, clutching a bowl of microwave popcorn. "Dang, cuz."

"I know. I look stupid."

"Are you kidding? It's hot. Just enough to make you innocently sexy. Virgin white with bedroom hair."

"Really?" She tugged at the open neckline of her dress. White, maybe, but virginal? "I don't have enough boobs to hold this up."

"It's fine. Quit fussing."

She didn't take his advice. She tugged at the neckline again. "At least I bought a shawl to cover up with." The evening wrap had been her idea, not the salesgirl's.

He plopped down on the edge of her bed and began stuffing his face with the popcorn, as if this were a movie he was watching on TV. "Covering up defeats the purpose."

She turned away from the mirror. "Do you have any idea how scared I am?"

"All you have to do is go to his club."

"You told me the other night that a man like him would fuck me raw."

"Yeah, I know. But the money isn't contingent on that. So just take that big fat donation and run."

"I don't think it's going to be that easy."

"What are you worried about, Jenny? That you're going to want to fuck him?"

"No."

"Liar. You know damn well you're attracted to him. Can't say as I blame you. If I was a chick, I'd do him."

"Jesus, Matt."

"I'm just saying."

"You could be a little more empathetic."

"What are you talking about? I helped you get yourself all gussied up, didn't I? I spent hours at the mall, and I hung around at that frou-frou salon, too."

Clearly, his definition of "empathetic" differed from hers. "You flirted with every female we encountered, including the sales-clerk and the stylist who mangled my hair. If the makeup artist had been a woman instead of a gay man, he would have been in your sights, too."

"I had to do something to keep busy." He ate another handful of popcorn. "I wonder what Noah's club is like. I'll bet it's really exclusive. It might even be at his house, maybe a Playboy Mansion–type place. Or it could be on a yacht. That would be kind of funny, huh? A dude named Noah with a big boat."

She rolled her eyes, and he laughed. She actually laughed a little, too.

Then she sighed. "You're right, Matty. I'm attracted to him."

"I know."

"I wish I wasn't."

"Figure it this way: If you consider the lengths he's going to in order to seduce you, you've got the upper hand."

"Him wanting me that much doesn't make sense."

"It makes sense to him."

"I'm not going to sleep with him." No matter how far or deep his seduction went, she was going to fight it. "He's too wild for me."

"That's fine. Just keep your cool. Being nervous won't solve anything."

She glanced at the clock. "It's only eight thirty. I got dressed too soon."

"So have some popcorn with me."

She sat next to him. "I can't eat anything." She bumped his shoulder. "But thanks for being here. I shouldn't have accused you of not caring."

"No problem."

"Will you stay until it's time for me to leave?"

"Sure, and if you start feeling freaked-out when you're there, call me and tell me where the place is, and I'll come get you."

"Thanks. That means a lot to me." It was as protective as Matt got.

The town car arrived at nine on the dot, and the driver came to the front door to get Jenny. He was a properly attired middle-aged man with a professional attitude.

Matt stood on the porch while she climbed into the backseat. He lifted his hand in a quick wave, and she was off to Lord knew where.

Once the driver embarked on the freeway and headed south, she looked out the window and reminded herself to breathe.

The final destination was downtown LA in a remote part of

the city. No restaurants. No people. No Playboy-type mansions. All she noticed were industrial buildings.

Finally the car stopped in front of a four-story structure surrounded by an iron fence. She suspected that it was a remodeled warehouse, and the way it had been redone gave it a distinctively Gothic vibe, with vaulted windows and decorative details. It even had gargoyles looming from the top of the building.

The driver climbed out from behind the wheel and opened her door. They stood on the sidewalk, and he handed her a key card for the gate.

"There's a lobby inside," he said. "Your host will see to you from there."

She assumed he meant Noah.

He continued by saying, "When it's time for you to leave, I'll be here to take you home."

She unlocked the gate and advanced forward, where a darkened archway led to the front door. Jenny felt like a dumb B-movie heroine walking into an obvious trap. Matt entertaining himself with popcorn was nothing compared to this. If she had an audience, they'd be sitting on the edges of their seats, waiting for her demise.

She opened the door and entered a dimly lit lobby. Victorian and medieval furnishings were mixed with modern Goth, creating a montage of scrolled woods, luxurious fabrics, and wrought iron twisted into menacing shapes.

A group of people, dressed like vampires, werewolves, and

creatures she couldn't quite name, gathered in front of a hotel-style desk. Jenny got in line behind them, assuming that was what she was supposed to do.

It was like Halloween on an erotic night.

Everyone who wasn't in costume was scantily attired. Even some of the costume-clad wore next to nothing. She removed her shawl to fit in a little better.

She glanced at the other side of the room and noticed a set of ornately carved double doors. A bouncer stood in front of them. He was as big as a mountain and as stoic as a Buckingham Palace guard. Music pounded in the background, coming from behind the doors, which got louder every time they were opened and someone was granted entrance.

The line dwindled and she made her way to the desk. The receptionist was blond, with enormous breasts crammed into a teeny-tiny see-through top. She also had a dazzling smile.

The greeting was a bright "Hello," followed by, "I just need to see your membership card."

Jenny handed her the key card. "I'm supposed to meet—"

The perky girl cut her off. "Gate keys won't get you into the club. You need a valid membership or guest pass."

"But Noah arranged it."

"Oh." A light dawned in the blonde's heavily lined eyes. "Then you must be Jenny."

"Yes."

"Noah told me to expect you. Hold on and I'll let him know

you're here." She stepped back and made a quiet cell phone call. Afterward, she said, "Just take a seat. He's on his way."

"Thank you." Jenny headed for a crushed velvet settee.

Noah soon arrived. He approached her, but it took her a moment to realize it was him. In fact, she just sat on the settee and stared.

He was in costume: part man, part mountain lion. His eyes, now gold with round black pupils, were completely reshaped to those of a cat. His nostrils were flared, and his long black hair was colored with tawny streaks, like the natural pelt of the animal he was imitating. He smiled, exposing long, sharp canines.

She didn't know much about special effects, but she was an expert on felids, and he looked outrageously authentic. Now she really felt as if she were part of a movie.

Transfixed, she finally stood up. She wanted to touch his face, to try to see how something so lifelike was possible, but she kept her hands to herself.

"You know more about mountain lions than you led me to believe," she said.

"Maybe I just know how to look like one. Speaking of looks, you're a feast for hungry eyes." He reached out to grasp a handful of her hair, feathering it between his fingers. "You're breathtaking, Jenny."

She tried to keep his compliment from affecting her. Worse yet was his touch. She almost leaned into him. He was frighteningly tempting. "I don't fit in here. I don't even understand what this place is."

"It's a supernatural-themed sex club. Some of us pretend to be mythical beings, and others present themselves as groupies."

She'd obviously been cast in the role of a groupie. "Does this club have a name?"

"It's called Aeonian. It means 'everlasting.' My office is on the fourth floor. My apartment is up there, too."

"You live here?" She couldn't fathom it.

"It suits me."

Silence stretched between them, and he touched her again. Only this time he trailed a neatly trimmed nail along her collarbone. Jenny wasn't sure how she was going to survive his allure.

"Want to see a party trick?" Without waiting for a response, he lifted his hand from her skin and bared his claws.

Yes, his claws. All ten nails burst forward in wildcat precision. He retracted them just as quickly.

Her head all but spun.

"I'm just a rich guy having some fun," he said.

A rich guy who could save her rescue. "Why did you pick me?"

"Pick you for what? My prey? Because you fascinate me. Because the thrill is in the hunt. Because victory is going to taste hot and sweet."

Goose bumps peppered her arms. "Do you even care about the cats? Or are they merely part of the game?"

"I care. I make anonymous donations to places like yours all the time. I've just never fucked anyone affiliated with them."

"You're not going to fuck me, either."

He ignored her denial. "You aroused me from the moment I first saw you."

Her heartbeat skittered. "Where did you first see me?"

"On your website. I was interested in more rescues to support and asked my accountant to do the research. He discovered that yours was the neediest and directed me to your site."

"So you decided to help me at a sexual price?"

"That wasn't my initial intention. But then I saw your picture and thought . . . why not?"

"You chose me based on how I look?"

"A lovely young zoologist with an affection for big cats who's struggling to keep her rescue afloat. I was too intrigued not to pursue you."

Could he be any more daring? And could she be any more vulnerable? "How long have you owned the club?"

"I opened it about five years ago."

"Have you been portraying a mountain lion all that time? Or have you worn other costumes?"

"This is it. But I'm not portraying the animal itself. I'm portraying a shapeshifter. There's a difference."

"What inspired you to create a supernatural theme?"

"A mysteriously beautiful woman in Mexico gave me the idea."

It was an evasive answer and far too intriguing. Jenny still had the urge to touch him, to marvel at how authentic he looked.

He said, "Before we enter the club, maybe I should tell you what to expect."

"You mean warn me?"

A feral smile appeared. "I suppose so."

She expelled an audible breath. She'd wanted to know what to expect from the beginning. "Go ahead."

"The first floor offers a retro-style disco, a host of bars, some quiet alcoves, and a BDSM dungeon."

She scrunched up her face. "Is that one of those places where people dress up in leather and use whips and chains?"

"It's more varied than that. BDSM is a consensual lifestyle that involves bondage and discipline, dominance and submission, and sadism and masochism. It doesn't necessarily include all of them, and the degree of activity and role-play varies."

"Are you into that?"

"It's not my lifestyle of choice, but sometimes I enjoy a bit of bondage." He paused. "Restraining you would be exciting."

"I don't . . . I'm not—"

"Not what? Interested in being tied to my bed?"

Noah bared his claws again, and Jenny tried not to flinch. This time his party trick seemed like a reflex. But after portraying the same character for so long, she assumed that his catlike behavior had become second nature.

He continued to brief her on the upcoming tour. "The second

floor is designed for voyeurism, and it's consensual, too. Everything that goes on here is."

She had to ask. "Do you participate in voyeurism?"

"I'm a good observer."

"What about being watched?"

"That can be fun, too. I'd put my paws all over you right now if you didn't look like your knees were about to buckle."

His paws? Was he trying to be funny? "My knees are fine."

"Does that mean I can caress you?"

And cut her to shreds? His claws were still bared.

He glanced down at his hands. "Oops. Sorry." He retracted the sharp points and moved closer. "How about now?"

She took a step back and bumped into the settee. "No."

"Too bad. I'm already half-hard thinking about it."

She fought the illicit temptation to sneak a peek at his fly. Luckily she was distracted by new activity in the lobby. Another group of club goers came in and headed for the desk. Jenny deliberately glanced their way. One of them was a woman costumed like a mermaid, with a bikini top fashioned from seashells that barely covered her nipples and an iridescent skirt that split at her ankles like a fin. She was long and lean and far too sensuous.

"Voyeurism suits you," Noah said.

Jenny snapped her attention back to him.

He tilted his head. "You focused on her to avoid looking at me."

She was still avoiding looking at him. Or at his fly, at least.

She trained her gaze above his belt. If he was half-hard, she wasn't inclined to find out.

Struggling to defend herself, she said, "Did you know that humans are the only predators mountain lions have?"

"Yes, but you rescue cats, not hunt them, so that doesn't pertain to you. Which reminds me, the first place I'm going to take you is the Animal Shifter Bar. It's on the main floor and is where my kind gathers."

She didn't want to think about him or his make-believe kind. "You never told me what's on the third floor."

"All sorts of creative activities. Food play, body painting, fake blood baths. The latter is a vampire ritual."

"The blood better be fake," she mumbled.

He responded with a click of humor. "The last time I checked, it was."

As he escorted her to the double doors, she took a big submerging breath, preparing to enter his bizarre domain.

Three

The main doors opened straight into the disco, with flashing lights and loud, wild music. In addition to the spinning strobes, black lights created ominous illuminations.

Jenny struggled to take it all in.

Clearly, your sexual orientation didn't matter and neither did your chosen breed. You were free to play, talk, laugh, and dance, as dirty as you saw fit.

Between the hot and hungry gyrations, the unfamiliar song blaring in her ears, and the mind-bending lights, her equilibrium was failing.

She clutched Noah's arm to keep herself steady. But it barely helped. As he led her through the disco and toward the Shifter

Bar, other women kept bumping against him, touching him purposely. He was, quite obviously, a groupie favorite. But why wouldn't he be? Not only was he gorgeously feral; he was megarich and he owned the club.

Aeonian and everything in it belonged to him. Jenny certainly felt as if she were a piece of his property. He held her future in his hands. She desperately needed the donation he was offering. Of course she wouldn't be here otherwise.

Finally they exited the disco and came to a quiet hallway that led to a door decorated with a variety of fur, feathers, reptile skins, teeth, claws, bones, and hooves.

Some of the pieces were faux and some had been derived from true animal sources, making the overall design a reminder of how odd this place was.

Noah opened the door and they went inside. Bathed in a misty light, the bar was packed with predators, with plenty of groupies to go around.

Jenny walked beside Noah, and all eyes turned in their direction. His godlike presence was even more pronounced here. He escorted her to a table in the back of the room with a "Reserved" sign on it. She took a seat and prayed this night would end with her sexual sanity intact. He sat next to her, close enough to touch her if he so desired.

At a nearby table, a woman whose naked body was expertly painted in the form of an eastern diamondback rattlesnake took the liberty of straddling a male groupie. She slithered up and down, rubbing against his bulging fly.

Jenny shifted her gaze to another table, where a cat-eyed man whispered to the female groupie beside him. She was blond, like Jenny, and he was dark, like Noah, only his hair was short and spiky and he wore studs in both ears. He had a pierced nose, too. Edgy as he was, he seemed enchanted by his groupie, and she seemed equally enthralled with him.

Jenny wondered if they were a committed couple, if they saw each other outside of the club. It was foolish, she supposed, to imagine them in a romantic relationship, but that was what she was doing.

Curious, she kept looking at them. Then, suddenly, the girl began unbuttoning the man's shirt, exposing a tattoo of a melanistic leopard on his chest. The leopard, or black panther as it was commonly known, was poised to strike, the ink strong and powerful against the man's skin.

Once his chest was fully bared, the groupie worked her way under the table and got between his legs. Although the tabletop covered the specifics, it didn't take a genius to know what was about to happen.

Too uncomfortable to watch, Jenny turned away, then locked gazes with Noah. In her delirium, she imagined putting her mouth on him, even though she'd never considered herself very good at performing that particular act.

He stayed silent for a moment.

Then he asked, "What are you in the mood for?"

Her pulse skipped. "What?"

"To drink?"

"I don't know." She couldn't think straight.

"Should I recommend something?"

"No, it's okay. I'll take a Bellini." She struggled to create a normal conversation. "I had one of those the last time I went out to dinner."

"Then you'll have one here, too."

Noah flagged down a waitress, who rushed to serve him. He ordered Jenny's cocktail. For himself, he requested extra-aged tequila, specifying the brand.

Within no time, their drinks arrived. Hers was in a tall glass, as expected, and his was presented in a faceted crystal snifter. She'd never seen anyone drink tequila from a snifter, but she didn't know anything about high-quality brands.

"Good?" he asked, after she tasted her Bellini.

She nodded and took another sip.

"They're an interesting pair," he said.

Her skin went hot. She knew he was talking about the tattooed man and his groupie.

He glanced in the vicinity of their table. "Their relationship is exclusive."

So they *were* a couple. "I don't want to talk about them." Let alone look at them.

"Then what should we talk about?"

"Nothing."

"You just want to sit here and listen to each other breathe?"

That wasn't her idea of nothing, especially with the invasion of her thoughts. She didn't want to imagine giving Noah oral sex. Yet her mind kept straying in that direction.

To combat the visual, she grabbed her cocktail and sucked hard on the straw, but the slushy drink didn't help. Her skin remained hot.

"Slow down," he whispered.

His voice was so soft and sensual, he could have been giving her blow job instructions.

Jenny needed to escape, to cool off, to put some water on her face. "Where's the ladies' room?"

"Over there."

All the way across the other side of the bar. Damn. Still, it was better than sitting here, thinking about putting her head in Noah's lap.

She stood up and pushed away from her chair. She had to weave her way around other tables to reach the aisle, but at least she was able to avoid the tattooed man and his lover.

Finally, she made it to the ladies' room and gazed at herself in the mirror. She looked positively haunted. Flushed, too. She wet a paper towel and dabbed it against her skin.

A trio of groupies came in to use the facilities and fix their makeup.

A snippy brunette joined her at the mirror and said, "What's wrong? Is Noah too much for you?"

Yes, Jenny thought. But she responded, "I can handle him just fine."

"Really? Well, did you know that some of the groupies think that Noah is a real shapeshifter?"

"No, I wasn't aware of that." But she wasn't surprised that people thought Noah was real. This club was a breeding ground for wacky superstitions and moonlit myths.

The haughty girl said, "I heard that he descends from an Inca god."

Jenny wanted to tell the little twit that he descended from the Seminole Tiger Clan, but she kept that information to herself.

The brunette finished her lipstick application, and she and her companions left.

Jenny cooled her face off again, tossed the paper towel in the trash, and exited the bathroom, only to be stopped by a man in a coyote mask.

"Good evening," he said.

She answered him cautiously. "Hi."

"You're with Noah tonight," he remarked.

She sighed. "Are you going to tell me that he might be a real shapeshifter, too?"

"I wanted to tell you that I'm his accountant."

Oh, goodness. "You're the one who directed him to my rescue?"

"Stanley Truxton. But I'm known as Coyote here."

She wished she could see his face rather than the mask he wore. Simple as it was, it covered everything except his mouth and chin.

He asked, "Who told you that Noah might be real?"

"A girl in the bathroom. She just rattled it off."

"Ah, yes. The rumors. But they aren't just about Noah. Other supernaturals are believed to be genuine, too." He smiled. "Not me, though. Can you imagine? An accountant turning into a coyote? And in a cheap mask, to boot."

"I can't imagine anyone turning into anything."

"If you ever start believing it, you can give me a call and we can discuss it."

Taken aback, she asked, "You think the rumors are true?"

"I know it sounds crazy, but I have proof that they are."

Crazy indeed. But what did she expect? He was a member of this club. "I think I should get back to Noah now."

"Certainly. But remember, if you ever want to talk . . ." He removed a business card from his pocket and handed it to her.

Anxious to get away from him, she slipped it into her purse. "Good-bye, Stanley."

"Coyote."

"Yes, Coyote." She darted off, making her way through the bar again.

She resumed her seat next to Noah and told him that she'd just heard about the rumors. She also mentioned the weird thing his accountant had said.

Noah shrugged. "He likes to mess with people's minds. He

portrays a coyote because they're tricksters. You can't trust what they do and say."

"Then why do you use him as your accountant?"

"He takes money seriously." He leaned into her. "The way I'm taking you as my prey seriously."

"That isn't funny." And neither was the urge he incited. She wanted to turn her head so he could kiss her. But she was afraid, too, fearful that his sharp-toothed kiss would hurt, fearful that it would feel good.

"I think you're ready to see the dungeon now."

The place where the bondage stuff was practiced?

She went with him, allowing him to take her wherever he wanted to go.

Noah thrived on the feeling of being with Jenny, of teasing her, of baiting her. It was especially thrilling when they reached the entrance of the dungeon.

"This isn't what I expected," she said.

"It's only the reception area." A room with a rustic bar, wrought-iron tables, and black leather sofas. "There's a lot more to come."

A handful of all-too-familiar groupies lingered about. Noah ignored them and took Jenny down a hallway with numbered doors.

"These are private playrooms," he said. "They have to be reserved in advance."

"Like a bondage hotel? It's all so strange."

"It's going to get stranger," he warned.

They turned a corner and headed down a long corridor, where medieval torture devices were bolted to the walls. Noah had acquired them from a warlock who'd time traveled from that era.

Approaching their final destination, he steered her toward a heavy wooden door. But he didn't open it. Instead, he prompted the moment to linger, allowing her curiosity to build.

"What's in there?" she asked.

"The community playroom." He waited a beat, then opened the door and took her inside.

The first sight that came into view was a beautiful blonde tied to a whipping pole. Jenny all but gasped.

Noah guided her farther into the room. It had been designed to represent a modern version of an old-style dungeon, with brick-walled chambers overflowing with public activity.

While masters dominated their slaves in the wildest of ways, candles burned, scenting the air with wax.

Noah put his hand on the swell of Jenny's back, doing his damnedest to keep his claws in check. He hungered to bare them, to slice her pretty white dress in half.

"Keep going," he told her. "There is a row of prison cells ahead."

On the way, they passed a fully aroused man being chained to an X-shaped cross. Jenny took a curious peek, then glanced quickly away.

Her shyness elevated the ambience, enhancing Noah's attraction to her. Sooner or later, he was going to strap her to his bed and make her come as roughly and perilously as he could.

The first prison cell was empty, and he nudged her toward it.

She gave him an uneasy look. "Don't lock me inside."

"I won't."

"Promise?"

"Yes." He entered the cell with her, leaving the door open.

Once they were standing side by side, she asked, "Have you ever been locked in one of these?"

He shook his head. "Just the thought of being caged up makes me uneasy."

"Actually, I'm okay with being in confined spaces."

He studied her. "Then why would it matter if I locked you in?"

"I didn't want to get trapped by you."

"You already are, Jenny. Maybe not in this cell, but in other ways."

"I'm trying not to be." She glanced at the prisoner next to them.

Noah glanced over, too. A female slave, delicately attired in a lace G-string, knelt over a portable bondage bench, waiting for her master to come in and spank her.

"I'm not going to take you to the voyeurism floor tonight," he said, changing the original plan.

Jenny seemed relieved. "Because I've seen enough already?"

"No." His goal was to make it more intimate. "There are bedrooms on that floor with private viewing areas and the next time you're here, we can watch with no else around."

"Watch what, exactly?"

"Anything that interests you. A couple, a threesome, an orgy. Something harsh or tender. You can decide, and I'll arrange it ahead of time."

"I don't even want to consider something like that."

"You will."

"I wish you'd stop telling me what you think I'm going to do." She bit down on her bottom lip. "I'm already nervous enough."

"Maybe I should kiss you to calm you down."

She bit a little harder. "You'll probably claw me."

"No, I won't."

"I don't trust you."

"Then you can kiss me. You can go at your own pace."

She inched forward, obviously intrigued.

He watched her come toward him, her expression a mixture of anxiety, curiosity, and attraction.

She got closer and he breathed her in.

"Such a sweet scent," he said.

"I'm not wearing a fragrance."

"It's just you. You're naturally sweet." Combined with the sex-infused, candlelit air, it drove him crazy.

"Mountain lions don't have an overly keen sense of smell," she said, going into chatty science mode. "Not compared to some of the other cats. Of course, compared to people, they do. But—"

For the hell of it, he took another whiff of her skin. "Come on and kiss me, Jenny. I won't bite."

"Don't make jokes, not now."

He wasn't. "Just do it."

She leaned forward and grazed his lips with hers. He could taste her pearly pink lipstick, and he imagined that it was the same soft shade as her clit.

He opened his mouth, inviting her to deepen the contact. She did, tentatively, but it was enough to make him fight for control. She was like a thirst-quenching stream on a sun-battered day.

How in God's name was he going to keep himself from devouring every luscious inch of her? He wanted to pull her tight against him and drag her to the ground.

Her tongue grazed one of his canines, and she shivered all the way to her bones, making him shiver, too.

Slap! Slap!

The sudden spanking of the prisoner next door destroyed the moment.

Jenny jumped back, and Noah cursed beneath his breath. Of all the fucking times for the master to paddle his slave's naughty little ass.

"What should we do now?" Jenny asked, as if the dungeon was about to catch fire.

"Let's go to the third floor." Frustrated, his claws popped out. While retracting them, he roughly added, "Where the blood baths are."

Four

As Noah took her to the third floor, Jenny's thoughts divided, caught between that soul-jarring kiss and the anticipation of the blood baths.

Once they reached the landing of the staircase and headed down a hallway, she relaxed a little. The area was brightly lit with a row of colorfully painted doors.

Determined to stay focused, she looked around and noticed a door with a big juicy apple painted on it. That seemed safe enough. She quickly asked, "What's in there?"

"It's the food play area. For people who have erotic fetishes that involve food. It's not a deep, dark fetish of mine, but I've dabbled in it." He snared her gaze. "I wouldn't mind eating something off of you."

Yikes. This wasn't a safe conversation, but apparently nothing about Noah was safe.

He continued, "I could rub chunks of pineapple on you and lick off the juice."

She imagined the sticky substance trailing between her thighs.

"Pineapple is one of my favorite treats," he told her. "I'm not a strict carnivore."

"I didn't think you were."

"I do like my meat rare, though." He gestured to a door splattered with red paint. "And speaking of carnivorous behavior, that's the blood bank, where vampires pretend to feed and where the baths occur."

She expected him to take her inside. Luckily, he didn't. She breathed a whopping sigh of relief.

He continued the tour. "Behind the sparkling blue door is the sensation center. That's where people use toys and sensory objects to stimulate themselves or their partners."

Jenny didn't comment. She didn't know anything about sex toys. She'd heard about parties where women got together to buy those kinds of items, sort of like Tupperware parties, only kinkier, she supposed.

Noah guided her farther down the hallway. "The art center is over there. It's for body painting and whatnot. I'm not skilled in that regard, but I appreciate art. That's why I included a museum on this floor, too. It's filled with erotic and supernatural-themed paintings and sculptures."

He didn't take her to the museum. He turned around and headed toward the blood bank. She slowed her steps.

"Come on," he coaxed.

Shoot. She moved forward. Lagging behind wouldn't earn her the check he was supposed to give her tonight.

He opened the red-splattered door, and she wished he didn't have such a strong hold over her. Between the money and her attraction to him, he'd snared her but good.

He ushered her into a cavernous room with sofas and chairs, occupied by groupies being fed upon. Jenny noticed that some of the players were more theatrical than others. A man with tousled dark hair and hypnotic green eyes sucked ravenously on a woman who actually looked as if she was in a trance. Her skin was almost as pale as his, and her head flopped back, exposing the column of her neck.

"This way," Noah said, taking Jenny in another direction.

They came to an area with tiled floors and rows of claw-footed bathtubs. It was creepier than she'd imagined.

More fake vampires.

Dressed in Gothic garb, they leaned over the tubs and poured thick red liquid from antique pitchers, drenching naked groupies.

In another area was a row of shower stalls for the bathers to rinse their skin after their experience ended.

Jenny stayed close to Noah, which did little to ease her discomfort. He'd created this setting for his club, and it looked like an erotic remake of *Psycho*.

The female groupie in the first tub was climaxing. She had her hand between her legs, stroking herself while she took her bath. The vampire dousing her with blood was female, too, and remarkably beautiful, with a shapely figure and long, fiery auburn hair. She glanced over at Noah and smiled.

"That's Sienna," he said.

Curious if they were lovers, Jenny asked, "Do you sleep with women who dress up as supernaturals?"

"No." He put his mouth close to her ear. "They don't make good prey."

"Not like me."

"No one is like you. You're my sexual ideal."

"Matt said that I have the upper hand."

"Who's Matt?"

"My cousin. He was at the fund-raiser. The man I was talking to before you approached me."

"Why does he say you have the upper hand?"

"Because of the lengths you're going to in order to seduce me."

"Hmm. That's interesting. So is he right? Does it make you feel powerful to know how badly I want you?"

She looked at the bloodied activity in front of her. "Not at the moment."

"I wonder if you'll feel powerful when you're strapped to my bed. Or when—"

She cut him off. "I want to go now."

"Go where?"

"Home." She needed to breathe, to get away from him.

"All right."

She spun around to face him. "You're going to seriously let me go?"

"Yes."

"And give me the check?"

"Yes," he responded again. "But you're going to go home and think about this place and me and the scenario you want to create for the second floor."

The voyeurism. "I don't have that kind of imagination."

"Sure you do. I'll bet by tomorrow morning, you'll have all sorts of ideas about what you'd like to see."

From the corner of her eye, she noticed Sienna's groupie heading for a shower stall. "It won't involve vampires."

"But it will involve somebody."

"I didn't mean it like that. You're tripping me up."

"So I am. Come on. I'll take you out of here."

Once they were in the hallway with the blood bank door securely closed, he handed her the check.

She didn't thank him, but he obviously didn't expect her to. The strings he'd attached to the money were tugging hard and deep.

When she got home that night, she stripped off her clothes, climbed into bed, and pressed a pillow between her legs, with Noah and his club swirling in her mind.

The following afternoon, Jenny worked her butt off, and she enjoyed it. She'd always thrived on running the rescue, but today she felt an exhilarating sense of freedom to go along with it. This place was hers to keep. No more worries about losing Big Cat Canyon.

Her only concern was Noah. She couldn't stop obsessing about him. She'd even fantasized about the voyeurism scenario, just as he'd said she would. But if she knew what was good for her, she would never return to his club. She would never see him again or talk to him or—

Her cell phone rang and she checked the screen.

It was Noah.

She struggled to ignore his summons, or better yet to push the "End Call" button, but she did neither. Within seconds, *mere seconds*, she lost the battle and answered with a customary, "Hello?"

"Sweet Jenny," came his reply. "Where are you?"

Her heart clamored to her throat. "Alone in my office."

"I'm alone in my apartment."

At this midday hour, she pictured him the way he looked

without the special effects. But he was wild either way, and his seduction ran deep.

"Have you been thinking about me?" he asked.

Lying seemed futile. "Yes."

"I've been thinking about you, too." A shot of silence; then, "What about the voyeurism scene? Any ideas about what you'd like to see?"

She should hang up now, before she went too far, but she tumbled further into his seductive trap. "Yes."

"Tell me."

She gazed out the blinds of a small paned window, where daylight scattered in front of her eyes. "A couple."

"What sort of couple?"

"I've been imagining specific people." She'd actually based her fantasy around real-life lovers. "The man with the tattoo and his groupie."

A smile sounded in Noah's voice. "Oh, that's good. They like being watched. I'm sure they'd be glad to perform in a private setting for us. So . . . what would you like to see them do?"

"I—" She couldn't bring herself to say it.

"Don't be shy. Just tell me whatever it is."

"I want—" She stalled again.

"You want what?" he pressed.

She didn't answer.

He persisted. "Jenny?"

She blurted it out. "I want to see her do to him what she was doing in the Shifter Bar."

"You want to watch her give him head?"

Her heartbeat tripled. "Yes."

"How do you want it to play out?"

"What do you mean?"

"What sorts of details have you envisioned? Do you want him to be fully naked? Half-clothed? Should he be standing? Sitting? Should she be kneeling in front of him? Or would you rather have both of them in bed, with him straddling her face? There are lots of ways it could happen."

Jenny squeezed her thighs together. She was getting warm down there. Far too warm. "I pictured him sitting in a chair beside the bed, with his jeans undone and his legs spread."

"What about her? How did you imagine her?"

"Kneeling on the floor, like she was at the bar."

"Is she clothed?"

"No. He made her strip before he told her to get on her knees."

"So there's a bit of domination involved? That's perfect, Jenny. Not only were you influenced by what you saw in the Shifter Bar, you're utilizing things you saw in the dungeon, too."

She rocked forward. Her panties were getting damp. "I also imagined him giving her instructions on how to pleasure him. To start off slow, then go deeper. I pictured him tangling his hands in her hair and looking down at her while she follows his commands."

"Were you touching yourself when you dreamed all of that up?"

"Yes." She'd been under the covers with her eyes closed, creating desperate longings. "I thought about it last night, soon after I got home. I tried to stop myself, but I couldn't. You'd already planted the seed."

He planted another one. "You should touch yourself right now. You should do it again."

She wanted to, but she made an excuse, trying to produce a semblance of reason. "I'm holding the phone."

He didn't back down. "Put it on hands free."

She made the switch. She got up and closed the blinds, too. Dizzy with need, she said, "I can't believe I'm going to do this with you on the other end of the line."

"That's what makes it so exciting."

She undid her khakis. "It makes me feel forbidden."

"I like that word."

At the moment so did she, but she was also deep under his spell and all mixed up. She slid onto her chair, grateful that he couldn't see her, yet wishing he could.

"Talk to me. Tell me exactly what you're doing."

"I'm sitting at my desk, tugging my pants and underwear down."

"What a visual. Sweet, sweet Jenny with her cunt exposed."

Heaven help her. "I'm unbuttoning my blouse, too. And unhooking the front of my bra."

"Are your nipples hard?"

"Yes." She drew a ring around one of them with her finger, making the areola pucker. With her skin tingling, with her mind on Noah, she moved her hand down and pressed it between her legs. "I'm going to do it now."

"Go right ahead."

She opened her nether lips and they glistened beneath her touch. "I'm already wet."

His voice caressed her. "Such a creamy girl."

Was she ever. She rubbed in little circles, spreading the warmth. Lost in the sensation and sealed in her own juices, her clit popped out.

"What are you thinking about?" he asked.

"You. Doing bad things to me."

"How bad?"

"You're restraining me, like you said you would do." While he listened, she made submissive sounds and envisioned being strapped to his bed.

"It scares me," she said, relaying her newfound hunger. "But I like it, too." In her fantasy, she was willing to let him tie her up. But in reality, she knew that she should stay away from him.

Still, she let herself dream, immersed in how hot and rough and carnal he was.

"Come for me," he said.

An instant inferno erupted in her belly, and she lifted her rear and thrust her hips, strumming hard and fast.

Come for him.

She moved in a carnal rhythm, rubbing her clit with one hand and using her other hand to push two fingers inside.

With Noah quiet on the other end, she gasped and went into spasms. She thrashed in her chair and bumped her knees against the desk.

Afterward, she blinked through the haze, the final shudder zinging through her blood.

"Jenny?"

She grabbled to right her clothes, fumbling with buttons, hooks, and fabrics that wouldn't behave. "Yes?"

"I'm going to arrange the voyeurism scene, and when the time is right, I'm going to restrain you, too."

She couldn't think to form a response. He'd given her barely a moment to breathe, let alone deal with an affair she shouldn't be having.

"Okay?" he prodded.

Overwhelmed, she agreed, allowing him to lure her back to the club and become part of his strangely erotic life.

In the middle of the night, Noah awakened in a state of confusion. He hadn't dreamed since he was mortal. But he'd just had one that involved Jenny, and it wasn't even sexual. He could've dealt with that. In fact, he would've welcomed it.

This was something altogether different. In his dream, the

magic stones the Seminole called *sapiya* had been hopping around on the ground and talking to him about Jenny.

He frowned into the dark. According to their message, he was supposed to show Jenny the beast that was inside him, to let her know the truth. Only the stones didn't explain their reasoning. They just kept insisting that he needed to do it.

Of all fucking things.

As a child, he'd been taught to respect the *sapiya*, because if you didn't, they could turn on you, if they so desired, and create bad magic. The way Noah saw it, he was screwed either way.

He stayed awake contemplating his dilemma, and by morning he was pacing his apartment like the caged hybrid he'd become.

Agitated, he grabbed his keys and headed out the door.

Twenty minutes later, he sat across from his accountant in the other man's high-rise office. In this environment Coyote was Stanley Truxton, a young, clean-cut CPA. But he was actually a shapeshifter, the same as Noah. Only Coyote was a trickster who wore a fake mask at the club instead of shifting into his half-animal form.

"What's going on?" Coyote asked.

Noah explained the details of his dream.

"Wow. You've gotten yourself into quite a predicament. Are you going to do it?"

"I don't know. But what damned difference does it make when you go around spouting that the rumors are real and claiming to have proof?"

"Don't turn this around on me. You know darn well that I only do that to have a bit of fun. Besides, hardly anyone at the club takes anything I say seriously. Most of the groupies think I'm a dweeb."

"Because you are."

The accountant laughed. "Isn't it a kick? A clever guy like me being a dweeb?"

Noah rolled his eyes. "I don't even know why I'm confiding in you."

"Who else are you going to talk to? A brainless werewolf or a flower-pollinating fairy? Or better yet, how about one of those snappy alligator shifters? Personally, I wouldn't trust those creatures as far as I could throw them."

"Look who's calling the kettle black." The only thing Coyote didn't screw around with was his clients' money. But Noah had known him a long time, and they were friends. Or as friendly as two detached beings could be.

"I wonder why the *sapiya* put you in a position like this?"

Noah scowled. "Hell if I know. All I want is to have a raging affair with her, and now those stones are digging a grave in my mind."

Coyote sat back in his chair, a view of the city framed in the picture window behind him. "Maybe Jenny is supposed to save you."

"What?"

"You know, like 'Beauty and the Beast.'"

"That's the goddamn dumbest thing I've ever heard."

"Actually, it's a lovely story. At the end Beauty saves Beast by telling him that she loves him." Coyote waggled his fingers. "Then—poof—he turns back into a handsome prince and they live happily ever after."

If the other man didn't already have such a scrawny little neck, Noah would've choked him. "I'm not a cursed prince, and this isn't a fucking fairy tale."

"It was just a thought."

"Not to me."

Coyote tapped his chin. "What if the *sapiya* create bad magic for Jenny? What if they turn on her instead of you?"

"Why would they do that?"

"Why wouldn't they? She was in your subconscious when they came rolling into your dream. She's just as much a part of this as you are."

"Shit." Noah wasn't going to willingly let something bad happen to her, and since he couldn't go back and undo that damned dream, he was hard-pressed to do what the magic stones said.

And unleash the beast.

Five

Nearly a week after the phone sex, Jenny stressed about Noah. She hadn't heard from him since that day and the anticipation was killing her.

Exhausted from taxing her mind, she plopped down on her sofa and turned on the ten o'clock news.

Halfway through the weather report, her doorbell rang. Because of the late hour, she rushed to answer it, concerned there might be an emergency at the rescue, something that was better dealt with in person than over the phone.

She flung open the door, and there stood Noah, in his full cat regalia, staring straight at her.

Jenny panicked. Had he come here to take her to the club?

"Is the voyeurism scheduled for tonight? You should have warned me that—"

He cut her off. "It's scheduled for tomorrow night."

"Oh, thank goodness. I don't think I could have been ready that quickly. I've been practicing how to do my own hair and makeup, and I bought a new dress to wear, but—" She halted, her train of thought changing in midsentence. "If we're not going to the club, why are you in costume?"

"Invite me inside, and I'll show you why."

She stepped away from the door. He seemed restless, and his mannerisms made her nervous. But when didn't he make her nervous?

As he entered the house that used to belong to her grandfather, she wondered what kind of impression it made on him. She'd added a few nice touches, like a wallpaper border in the kitchen and a cozy area rug in the den, but mostly she'd kept the outdated furniture and battered ranch accents.

She attempted to be a proper host. "Can I get you something?"

He motioned to the TV. "You can turn that off and sit down."

She punched the remote and the screen went black. She sat in her grandpa's old recliner and gestured to the sofa for him.

"I'd rather stand."

She waited for him to make the purpose of his visit known, but he merely stood in the center of her living room, looking at her.

"You're scaring me," she said.

"I've scared you from the start."

"I know, but you're acting strange."

"Stranger than usual?"

She shifted in her seat. "Yes."

He lowered his chin, making his catlike features more pronounced, and then he growled, the slow rumble vibrating from his throat. Jenny gripped the armrests on the recliner. He sounded *exactly* like a mountain lion.

Another party trick? He was too damned good at them.

"What are you doing, Noah?"

He snarled and moved closer.

"Stop it. This isn't funny."

He snarled again.

As Jenny struggled to make sense of his behavior, the do's and don'ts of a mountain lion attack swirled in her mind: don't run and allow it to give chase; remain standing if you can and try to meet the cat face-to-face; go for its eyes or pound your fists into its head; if at all possible, find something to use as a weapon.

Did those same rules apply to a crazed man mimicking a wildcat? Or would it behoove her to turn tail and run?

His claws popped out, and she jumped up, adrenaline bursting through her veins.

She glanced around for an object to hit him with, but there was nothing within her reach. The lamp was on the other side of the room. Doing the next best thing, she balled up her fists and swung at him.

He didn't take her aggression well. He grabbed her wrists and pushed her back onto the chair, where it snapped into a reclining position. Slamming his body on top of hers, he pinned her beneath him, making it impossible for her to move.

Only he didn't sink his teeth into her flesh or claw viciously at her clothes. Right in front of her, his features began to change, turning from cat to man.

Within seconds, his eyes went back to normal, along with his teeth, his nails, and his nostrils. Even the tawny streaks in his hair disappeared.

Stunned, Jenny merely lay there, staring at him. That was a party trick that seemed impossible. Yet he'd accomplished it.

He released her and stood up.

Although she moved the chair forward and got to her feet, she was far from steady. She wobbled like one of those roly-poly toys she used to play with as a kid.

Noah looked completely poised.

"Was that an illusion?" she asked. "Did you do that with mirrors or a camera or whatever it is that magicians do?"

"It was real."

"Can you turn back into a cat just as easily?"

"Yes."

Gathering her composure, she lifted her hands and put them against his face. "Then do it. Right now. With me touching you."

Just like that, he returned to lion mode, his features rippling and changing beneath her fingers.

Jenny was too fascinated to let go. She kept her hands on his face, even after his transformation was complete. But he didn't allow it to last.

He nudged her away. "The show is over."

She gazed into those animalistic eyes. He was like a science project gone powerfully wrong. "You can't just spring something like this on me and say it's over. I want to know more about you. I want to know how any of this is possible."

"It's possible because I'm a real shapeshifter."

"Yes, but how is *that* possible? Is it because of the woman in Mexico? The one you called beautiful and mysterious?"

"I don't want to talk about her."

She persisted. "You told me that she gave you the idea to be a shapeshifter."

"I was being facetious."

"So she wasn't involved?"

In lieu of a reply, he shifted back to human form, putting her emotions on edge and making her dizzy.

"I'll send the town car for you tomorrow," he said.

That was it? She was just supposed to come back to the club and let him dictate the terms of their affair? "I want answers."

"And you'll get them when I'm ready to discuss it."

He headed for the door, and she followed him onto the porch.

Before he left, he reached out and pressed his fingers against her neck, taking a moment to feel her pulse. It went rickety beneath his touch, proving that she was still his prey, no matter what identity he chose.

The next night, Jenny walked beside Noah at Aeonian, reprimanding herself for wanting to be here. But honestly, how could she stay away, knowing what she knew about him?

Tonight he was in lion form, as she'd expected him to be, but she was well aware of how easily he could change if the mood struck him.

They proceeded to the second floor, and he escorted her to a private viewing area and locked the door. It was a small space, dimly lit, with a floor-to-ceiling window that displayed a bedroom on the other side.

"The couple you requested will be arriving soon," he said.

She refused to pretend that her mind wasn't elsewhere. "I'm more interested in you."

"We'll deal with your curiosity about me later." He gestured to the window. "That's a one-way mirror, glass on our side and a mirror on theirs. So basically, we'll be able to see them, but they won't be able to see us, even if they know we're here."

Like in police interrogating rooms?

He beckoned her. "Come over here and face the glass so we can wait for Vince and Allison to arrive."

She moved forward. "Those are their names?"

"Yes, but don't ask me if he's a real shapeshifter because I'm not going to tell you."

"Are animal shapeshifters the only supernaturals who are real? Or do vampires and things like that exist, too?"

"Pretty much everything you can fathom exists. I built this place as a party spot for supernaturals to blend in without being recognized."

"It boggles my mind."

"Then stop thinking about it and concentrate on being entertained."

He stood behind her, and his breathing fluttered across her bare shoulders. She'd worn a strapless, slit-up-the-sides dress as her faux-groupie outfit, and he was making good use of it.

"What do you think of the bedroom?" he asked.

"It's beautiful." A winged-back chair was positioned next to a luxuriously draped bed. "Was the chair already in there? Or was it provided to suit my fantasy?"

"It was placed there for you."

"I can't believe I'm standing here, knowing what's going to happen, knowing it's something that stemmed from my imagination."

"We won't be able to hear Vince and Allison talking to each other. But rest assured, he'll be saying the kinds of things you'd want him to say."

Butterflies erupted in Jenny's stomach. Not only was she

anxious about the voyeurism; she was anxious that she was locked in a viewing room with a man who was half mountain lion.

Nothing had ever felt so surreal.

A heartbeat later, the other couple entered the bedroom, and she gazed at them through the glass.

Vince had the same cat-shaped eyes as before, and he was shirtless, his tattoo clearly visible. Although Allison was fully clothed, she wasn't dressed like a groupie, not even a faux one. Her modest attire was similar to what Jenny had worn at the fundraiser. Even her hair was clipped into a ponytail with a simple gold barrette.

"Why did you make her look that way?" she asked.

"Because I couldn't help but toss in a bit of fantasy for myself." Noah slipped his arms around her. "I want to watch her and imagine that she's you getting on your knees for me."

She nervously admitted, "That's how this whole fantasy got started, with me thinking of doing it to you. Only I'm not very skilled at it."

"Is that why you wanted Vince to give Allison instructions?"

She went pliable in his arms. "Yes."

He tightened his hold on her, and together they watched the scene unfold.

Vince sat in the chair and opened his legs, getting into a slightly slouched position. It made him look madly erotic, especially when he undid the top snap on his jeans.

He spoke to Allison, and Jenny assumed that he was telling

her to strip. Sure enough, the modestly attired blonde began removing her clothes. She did it shyly, just the way Jenny would have, fumbling with her blouse and bra and nearly getting the zipper stuck on her skirt.

As she shed her panties, Noah's breathing quickened.

Vince made a circular motion, and Allison turned all the way around, showing him every angle of her naked body.

Ready for more, Vince opened his fly all the way, revealing his half-hard cock.

Jenny went warm all over.

Noah said, "I don't know how much of this I'll be able to take without fucking you."

She went full-blazes hot.

He continued, "We could do it right here, with me behind you and you pressed against the glass. All you have to do is tell me you want it."

Her fantasy took a dangerous turn. To stop herself from giving him permission, she gazed at the other couple. Vince was making Allison get on her knees.

Jenny's breath rushed out. Behind her, Noah was hard, his cock pressed against her bottom.

By now, Allison was crawling between Vince's knees. He opened his legs even wider, thrusting his penis toward her. She didn't touch him, though. She waited for him to give her instructions.

Jenny imagined that his voice was soft and low, with a roughened edge. To her, he would sound like Noah.

Then Noah spoke, giving her goose bumps. He said, "I wasn't sure if you wanted him to come in her mouth or pull out and spill it down the front of her."

A shudder wracked her spine. "Which way is it going to happen?"

"I left it up to them. For the mystery."

A wild mystery. Vince undid the barrette in Allison's hair, freeing her proper ponytail and running his hands through her blond tresses.

Noah nuzzled the back of Jenny's neck. He wasn't playing fair. She tried to focus on the other couple again.

At Vince's obvious command, Allison licked the crown of his cock, swirling her tongue with ladylike precision.

"They look good together," Noah said.

Far too good. Far too hedonic.

Just then, Allison took Vince in her mouth, and he pushed forward, fully aroused and insistent. Without thinking, Jenny leaned closer to the activity.

"Are you excited?" Noah asked.

Her pussy clenched. "Yes."

"Let me fuck you," he whispered, using the voice from her fantasies. "Let me fuck you while he fucks her mouth."

She struggled to think about something else, but she couldn't. Between the hard, hot fellatio and the craving Noah incited, she was losing it.

He told her, "If you don't say no, I'm going to do it."

One simple word. That was all it would take to refuse him. Yet Jenny remained silent.

A moment ticked by.

Noah lowered her dress, making it shimmy down her body and pool at her feet.

"Step out of it," he said.

She obeyed him, just as Allison continued to obey Vince. In and out he went, using her mouth for his pleasure.

"Your panties are next," Noah said.

Once again, all she had to do was tell him no. But it went unspoken. He peeled away what was left of her modesty.

As he stood behind her and roamed his hands along her curves, she gazed at Allison's naked body. The other woman remained on her knees.

Noah reached between Jenny's legs and probed the wetness. There was no denying that she was ready for him. She put her hands on the glass to brace herself.

The activity in the bedroom changed. Vince made Allison slow down, prolonging his orgasm.

Noah unzipped his pants, and the rasp of his zipper created a prominent sound amid the silence.

"I'm not going to use protection," he said. "Normally I do, but since you know what I am, it isn't necessary to pretend that it matters. Exchanging body fluids with me won't harm you."

Jenny had never had sex without a condom, and the notion of being flesh to flesh, especially with someone who wasn't altogether human, was strangely thrilling.

He entered her, mimicking the motion of Vince and Allison. Jenny fanned her fingers. Within the fraction of a heartbeat, Noah was purring.

The tips of her breasts grew taut under his touch. Her blood simmered. Her thoughts dazed. He increased the tempo, moving at a powerful pace. As if on cue, Vince urged Allison to resume a hard, fast sucking.

Noah braced himself against the window, too, but he was no longer purring. The noise he made was much more dangerous, a cross between a masculine groan and catlike hiss.

She pushed back against his ferocious thrusts, and he bared his claws.

Vince glanced up for a second. Had he heard Noah scratching against the glass? Whatever the case, he maintained his greedy position, with his legs widespread and Allison on the ground before him. She sucked and sucked, taking him all the way to the back of her throat. He was even holding her there, making damn sure she swallowed every inch.

The air in Jenny's lungs whooshed out. Noah was full hilt, too, literally fucking her breathless.

"Turn your head."

She struggled to respond. "What?"

"So I can kiss you."

She thought about how sharp his canines were, but she did his bidding, giving herself over to him.

His kiss was rough and demanding, and although he didn't bite her, it was touch and go, with his tongue darting in and out of her mouth and his teeth nearly clipping her.

This time, Jenny ran her nails along the glass. But Noah didn't. He managed to retract his claws.

Then, suddenly, he withdrew and swung her around, putting them face-to-face.

"What's wrong?" she asked.

"Nothing."

He reentered her, and she went lustfully mad. He was teasing her, keeping her away from the voyeurism. He could see the other couple, but she couldn't.

Noah clutched her ass and squeezed her cheeks. She wrapped one leg around him to keep herself steady. Or maybe it was to get closer to him, to fuse her undulating body to his.

"Vince is coming," he said.

So was Jenny. Every cell in her body raged.

"Tell me how," she pleaded. "Tell me."

He didn't reveal the mystery.

As Jenny went crazy and climaxed, she imagined it both ways, with Vince spilling into Allison's mouth, then pulling out to splash the rest of it on her.

Noah kissed Jenny one last time, and he came, too, emitting a soft, sensual growl and drenching her with white-hot liquid.

Afterward, his shapeshifter image spun before her eyes. By the time she summoned the strength to grab her clothes off the floor and turn around, Vince and Allison were gone.

Leaving nothing but an empty bedroom.

Six

B eing with Jenny was absolute nirvana.

And now that it was over, Noah wanted to pull away, to disengage himself from the feeling. But he couldn't, not completely. So he took her to his private quarters, preparing for the inevitable discussion.

But first he offered her a quick tour of the apartment: a spacious living room, two luxurious bedrooms, two bathrooms, a kitchen, a dining room, a media room, and a cantilever balcony in his bedroom that overlooked the city. He also had a rooftop pool and Jacuzzi, but he didn't take her up there.

As soon as they were back in the living room, she asked, "Why did you tell me the truth about yourself? Was it to scare me? To make me more interested in you? Or is it because of my background of working with cats?"

He hated to admit this part. "It was because of what the *sapiya* said to me in a dream."

"The *sapiya*?" she parroted.

"They're magic stones, and that's what they're called in my culture. But you have to be careful how you treat them. If you don't respect their medicine, they can turn on you." He frowned. "They told me that I was supposed to show you what I am, that you were supposed to know the truth. But I don't know why."

"I can't imagine why, either." She went quiet for a second, as if she were contemplating the situation. "But there must be a reason."

He wasn't about to mention the romantic crap Coyote had drummed up. "I only did what they told me to do because I didn't want them causing something bad to happen to you."

She seemed surprised. "You were concerned about protecting me?"

He shrugged. He didn't want her making a big deal of it. "The *sapiya* are strange little objects. They can jump around like fleas and multiply by themselves. They don't normally appear in dreams, and I've never owned any of them, so it's weird that they took an interest in me."

"How does someone own them?"

"You have to catch one, and once you have it, it has to be watered with fresh dew and fed with animal blood."

"Why would someone want the responsibility of owning a *sapiya* if they're so temperamental?"

"Because they can be used to attract other people to you. They can bring anyone you want to your door. But I wasn't asking for their help."

"Yet in a sense, they brought me to your door. Am I supposed to go home later? Or am I spending the night?"

"Do you want to stay?"

She nodded. She seemed to be getting more comfortable around him, and he wasn't sure if he liked it. He preferred to keep a bit of edge between them.

He knew he should send her home, especially with the unsolved *sapiya* motive lingering in the air, but he found himself saying, "You can stay."

"Is it all right if I take a bath? I need to clean up after what we did."

Sticky sex. "Yeah, me, too. You can use the guest bath, and I'll use the master."

She looked disappointed. Was she hoping to climb into the tub together and wash each other's backs?

Noah didn't alter the plan. He familiarized her with the guest bath and its complimentary toiletries. The soap was fresh milled, the shampoo was lemon scented, and the pre-pasted toothbrushes were disposable.

He got her some fresh towels and handed her a flowing red robe with the Aeonian logo. "You can keep it if you'd like to have it."

"Thank you. It's beautiful."

"Why don't we meet in the kitchen after we bathe? We can have a nightcap."

"I'm not really in the mood for alcohol. Do you think we could have hot chocolate or something like that?"

"I've got herb tea."

"I want to keep talking, too. I want to know how you became a shapeshifter."

"I know. We'll get to that."

He left and went to the master bath. Returning to his human form, he got in the shower and scrubbed clean.

About five minutes later, he shut off the water. As the steam dissipated, he dried off, slicked his hair back, and slipped on a thick cotton robe.

Wrapped in the dark, heavy fabric, Noah arrived in the kitchen first, but Jenny soon followed, soft and elegant in the crimson silk.

"You look the part," he said.

"What part is that?"

"Mistress of the immortal manor."

Her hair, slightly damp at the ends, waved softly around her face, and a slight residue of mascara remained on her eyes. "Is that what I am?"

"For tonight, I guess you are."

A second later, she asked, "Just how immortal are you?"

"What do you mean?"

"Are you actually going to live forever?"

"I haven't died yet."

"How old are you?"

"A hundred and sixty. Give or take a few."

She gaped at him. "I assumed that you became a shapeshifter around the time you opened the club."

"You assumed wrong." He retrieved the tea. As he riffled through the box, he made an uncharacteristic journey back to his youth. "We used to drink sofkee when I was growing up."

"What's that?"

"A beverage made from corn, hominy, rice, arrowroot, or grits, and boiled down into a hot soup. It was served at every meal. We drank it in between meals, too. My descendants are probably still drinking some form of it."

She got bright-eyed. "Can we make some?"

He should have kept his mouth shut. "Let's just have tea and forget it."

"I'll bet there's a modern recipe online we can follow." She dashed off to get her cell phone, which she'd apparently left in the bathroom with her purse and clothes. She returned and started looking around online. "How about this? It uses rice and cornstarch."

"I don't have any cornstarch."

She found another recipe. "This one uses baking soda. Do you have that?"

Would she keep trying until the right ingredients appeared in his cabinet or until she finagled a trip to an all-night market to get them? "Yes, I've got that."

Against his better judgment, he agreed to help her with the recipe.

They brought the water and baking soda to a boil and added the rice.

"It says to let the rice overcook," she said. "So the sofkee is the consistency of runny oatmeal."

"This isn't going to be the big cultural experience you're expecting," he warned. "You're going to think it tastes like shit."

"I'm having sex with a hundred-and-sixty-year-old shape-shifter who drank it when he was young. I have a right to be curious. Besides, I'm the mistress of the manor, remember? Tonight is my night."

"You're going to wish you opted for the tea."

She ignored him and went back to the recipe. "It says that you're not supposed to add salt, pepper, or other seasonings or it won't be genuine sofkee."

"We used to make another hot drink from boiling tomatoes with summer fruits and sweetening it with sugar."

"Really? That sounds good."

"Yeah, well, too late. We've already got the rice goop going." He reached for two coffee mugs, and when the sofkee was ready, he ladled it into the hearty containers and handed her one.

She took a small sip. "It's nice. Bland. Easy on the stomach." She went for another sip. "I actually kind of like it."

It tasted like home to him, making him too damned aware of what he'd lost.

"Can we drink this in bed?" she asked.

He gripped his cup. "I guess."

They entered his room, and he removed his robe, got into bed, and draped the sheet across his lap. She got under the sheet, too, but she kept her silky garment on. Both of them sat upright, with pillows propped behind their heads. He could feel her looking at him.

She asked, "How old were you when you became immortal?"

"Twenty-eight."

"That's how old I am, only I'll be turning twenty-nine next year and you won't." She went pensive. "So what's the story? How did it happen?"

"It was the woman in Mexico. She blazed into the cantina one night and flirted with me. I followed her outside, and we went into the woods and ravished the hell out of each other. After we fucked, she turned into a mountain lion and attacked me."

Jenny set her sofkee on the nightstand. "A half lion like you are now or a full-blown lion like the felids at my rescue?"

"She was like your cats, only different because of her ability to become human." He forged ahead. Now that he'd started this, he wanted to finish it. "It was quick and brutal, but it seemed as if it was happening in slow motion. I could feel her ripping into my flesh. I could even feel my blood streaming down my body and staining the ground. I tried to fight her off, but there was nothing I could do to stop her. I blacked out, and when I came to, it was morning and I was slashed to bits and staring at the sun, nauseous and confused." He paused. "I passed out again, and the next time I woke up, I was being treated by the local doctor. He had a little room in his house that served as his clinic. Someone had found me and brought me there."

"Did you tell the doctor what happened?"

"That the animal that mauled me was a shapeshifter? He would have thought I was delusional. Or possessed or Lord knows what else. I already looked like a monster, swollen, bruised, and broken, and my chances of survival seemed slim. I think the doctor was hoping for my sake that I didn't make it. My body was viciously scarred, and my face was horribly disfigured. I was unrecognizable, even to myself."

She studied him in the silence. Was she picturing him that way?

He carried on. "I finally got well enough to leave. I still looked like something that came out of the depths of a nightmare, but I was alive and able to function on my own."

"What did you do?"

"I went into the hills and lived like a leper. But little by little, I started to change. My scars began to heal and my face turned smooth again, and I sensed that I was becoming immortal. Then other things began happening, too. Catlike things."

Jenny tugged her robe closed, where it gapped, exposing one of her breasts. "You started shifting?"

He nodded. "But I never shifted all the way, not like the woman who mauled me. I could feel my body wanting to go there, to become a full-blown lion, but I fought it. I think I was able to stave it off because of my Tiger Clan affiliation. Or 'mountain lion medicine,' as it were. That protected me."

"Do you still get the urge to shift all the way? Do you still have that internal battle?"

"No." He finished his drink. "That only happened in the beginning."

She cocked her head, obviously still wanting to know more about him. "Where are you from, originally?"

"Indian Territory. Oklahoma," he clarified. "But it wasn't a state then."

"How does Mexico fit into your life?"

"It's part of my upbringing, too. My family migrated to Mexico from Indian Territory when I was a wee thing. We'd gone there with a band of other Seminoles, and we lived there for about ten years. Eventually the entire band returned to Indian Territory. But as an adult, I would make trips back to Mexico."

"And it was on one of those trips that you were attacked?"

He nodded. "After I became a shapeshifter, I never saw my family again. I didn't see how I could resume my life in Indian Territory and remain young while everyone else grew old around me. So I stayed in Mexico. Of course not in the town where I'd been attacked. I couldn't just show up looking right as rain after I'd drifted off with a disfigurement."

"Do you ever miss being mortal?"

He didn't like the question. But the answer was worse. "I did at first, especially when I thought about my family. But then I started to forget what they looked like, the sounds of their voices, everything that humans hold dear about their loved ones. It just faded away."

"I'm sorry, Noah."

Her sympathy hit him like another mauling, only without the teeth and claws. "I don't want to talk anymore."

"I didn't mean to—"

"Just never mind. It's time to sleep. Take off your robe, and I'll turn out the lamp."

She removed the garment and draped it over a post on the headboard. "I don't normally sleep naked."

"And I rarely allow my lovers to stay in my room."

"You have sex with them, then send them to the guest room?"

"Or send them home." Which was what he should have done with her.

She turned onto her side, facing him in the dark. Or the near darkness. He could see her hazy outline, where a smidgen of light spilled in from the balcony. If he craved a clearer view, all he had to do was morph into lion form and use his nocturnal vision. But he remained human.

Then her voice drifted over him. "Noah?"

"What?"

"What did the woman in Mexico look like?"

"I already told you that she was beautiful."

"And mysterious, I know. But what does that mean in terms of how she looked?"

He didn't figure where any of this mattered. "It means she was hot, bold, and fuckable."

"You don't have to be so evasive."

Screw it. He shifted into a lion so he could see her the way he wanted to see her. "What part of hot, bold, and fuckable is evasive?"

"All of it."

He stared at her. She looked sweet and tender, a predator's dream.

Her voice quavered. "Did you just shift?"

"How can you tell?"

"Your eyes are glowing."

He grinned. "You don't say."

As if to counteract his smugness, she went scientific. "Mountain lions have large pupils with rods for gathering light, and behind each retina is a reflective membrane."

"So that's why they're glowing? From catching the light from outside?"

"Yes."

"Her eyes were glowing when she attacked me."

She clutched the sheet closer to herself. "Are you trying to scare me?"

"You asked me what she looked like."

"I meant when she was human."

"And I told you to go to sleep."

She didn't respond, and Noah stayed awake until she got the guts to crash out beside him. He was tempted to touch her, maybe even tie her to the bedposts while she slept, but he kept his hands to himself.

Making the dawn of the next day that much more exciting.

Seven

Jenny awakened with a sunlit creature hovering over her. She blinked and got her bearings. Noah, surrounded by daylight, naked as the day he'd been turned into a shapeshifter and staring right at her.

"What are you doing?" she asked, realizing that the top sheet was gone, and she was as exposed as he was.

His gold eyes locked onto hers. He'd been a lion when she'd fallen asleep last night and he remained a lion this morning. "I'm watching you."

"Why?"

"I'm trying to decide whether to kiss you roughly on the lips or sweetly on the cunt."

Her heart bumped dreamily against her chest, belying the hot, thudding pulse between her legs. "You can do either one."

"Maybe I should restrain you first." He reached into the nightstand drawer and produced two silk bondage ties. "I considered tying you up while you were asleep, but that wouldn't have been very consensual of me."

She could only imagine the crazy dream she would've had. Then again, crazy dreams were part of the experience. She wouldn't have known that he was immortal if his dream hadn't intervened.

He didn't tie her to the bedpost. He just kept looking at her, drilling her with his primal gaze.

"What are you waiting for?" she asked.

"To see if you panic."

"Just do it." Before her heart beat its way out of her chest and into his devious arms. If anything was making her panic, it was the way she was starting to feel about him. The emotional attachment that was sure to get her into trouble.

"I'd rather keep you waiting." Teasing her, he put the restraints away. "We'll play bondage another time."

Frustrated, she moaned beneath her breath. "Are you still going to kiss me?"

"I might."

"Are you trying to make me beg?"

"I'm just enjoying the moment." He stretched like the cat he was and shifted back to human form.

"You make me dizzy when you do that."

"I can't help what I am."

Recalling their conversation from last night, she thought about the woman who'd turned him into a lion. "I still want to know what she looked like."

"So, we're back to discussing her?"

"You can't fault me for being curious. Women always wonder about other women, even under normal circumstances."

"She was a brunette, curvy, with ample tits and a big, lush ass." He leaned on his elbow. "Is that descriptive enough?"

Coming from him, the details didn't sound all that different from "hot, bold, and fuckable."

"Are there more out there like her?"

"More what?"

"Mountain lion shifters who maul people?"

"If there are, I'm not aware of them. In fact, the only lion shifters I've ever heard of are called 'Sky Dwellers,' but they live in the sky with an Inca god and are forbidden to interact with humans."

"How did they become shifters?"

"They were created that way."

"Is that how the rumors at the club got started that you descend from an Inca deity?"

He nodded. "Mountain lions were revered in that culture. The city of Cusco is said to be shaped like one, and if you look at a map of that region, it certainly seems so."

Jenny didn't know much about Cusco, except that it was in

Peru. "If a Sky Dweller came to earth, could it turn someone into what you are?"

"Not according to their legend. The reason they're forbidden to interact with humans is that a Sky Dweller and a human could never mate. Their bodies are poisonous to each other and the union would kill both of them. But some of the groupies at the club think that the legend is inaccurate and that I'm the offspring of a mortal woman and a Sky Dweller."

Now Jenny was even more curious about the shifter who'd mauled him. "If the woman who attacked you wasn't a Sky Dweller, then what was she?"

"I don't know."

"Have you ever tried to research her origins or find out more about her?"

"At the time I assumed she was from Mexico, but I didn't look for her after I recovered. I'm not like the vampires are with their makers. I don't feel a connection to her, and what's done is done. I can't change it."

"Did she at least tell you her name?"

"I asked who she was, but she didn't say. And by the time I followed her outside, I didn't care if her name was Diablo. All I wanted was to be inside her."

"She tore you up like a devil."

"Yeah, but before she mauled me, it was the best fuck of my life." He roamed his gaze over her nakedness. "Until last night when I fucked you."

She wanted to believe him. She wanted to be the best lay of his hundred and sixty-something years, but she had no way of knowing if he was being honest. "You're good at seducing me."

"And you're good at being seduced."

Her skin tingled. "Kiss me, Noah."

He didn't do it.

Her voice went raspy. "Please."

"What a contradiction you've become. In the beginning you insisted that you weren't going to be with me, and now you've resorted to begging."

Jenny didn't respond. But what could she say? He was right. Everything was turning on its ear, and God help her if she made the mistake of getting more and more attached to him.

He finally kissed her, slanting his mouth across hers, the flavor of his hunger overwhelming her. She wrapped her arms around him and held tight. They rolled over the bed and landed in the exact same position, with him on top of her.

He worked his way to her breasts and licked one of her nipples. It peaked under his touch. He blew on the spot, intensifying the sensation. He did the same thing to her other nipple. She put her hands in his hair, and he moved lower and tongued her navel.

Hot agony. She wanted him to eat her so badly, she arched her hips. Noah continued to lave her belly button, taking his sweet time.

Should she resort to begging again?

"Do it," she said.

He glanced up at her. "Do what?"

"Kiss me there."

"Where's there?"

Damn him for teasing her. She opened her legs, desperate to feel the heat of his tongue on her clit. She put her finger on the oh-so-sensitive spot. "Here."

"Why should I?"

"Because I need it." She thought about how it would feel to go down on him, too. To have him thrust hotly into her mouth, the way Vince had done to Allison.

He lingered at her navel. "They say patience is a virtue."

She moaned. "What do 'they' know?"

"I think it depends on who 'they' are."

She did the pleading thing again. *"Noah."*

"Maybe just one kiss." He put his lips against her clit, and Jenny bucked on contact.

It was more than one kiss. It was the warmest, slickest, sexiest feeling in the world. He slid his tongue along her labia, making her juices flow, and if she hadn't been so turned on, she would've been embarrassed about the way she was trying to rub her cream in his face.

Not that he seemed to mind.

He lifted her legs onto his shoulders and spread her wider. He was turning her into a maniac, and she thrived on the insanity. She watched his tongue glide in and out of her pussy, mimicking the motion of honey-drizzled sex.

His ministrations got stronger, and she tugged at the sheet. Everything was centered at her cunt.

Her heart. Her soul. Her dirty mind.

Once again, she was thinking about sucking him. She even imagined how powerful his ejaculation would be and how it would fill up her mouth before she swallowed it.

While he licked ravenously at her clit, Jenny lost it. Her orgasm burst like a geyser, leaving her limp when it was over.

He released her, and she could barely move. She couldn't believe the effect he had on her, not just sexually, but emotionally.

"Are you okay?" he asked.

"I'm fine." She regained the strength of her limbs and curled up against him, wanting to be close.

He cuddled with her, stroking a hand down her back. Jenny sighed, warm in his embrace. But it ended as quickly as it began. He pulled away, as if he realized what he'd done, as if being affectionate with her were a crime.

"You should get ready to leave now," he said.

She frowned. "Why?"

"Because you've been here all night, and it's time to go. As soon as you're dressed, I'll contact my driver to take you home."

"When are we going to get together again?"

"I'll call and let you know."

Her romantic bubble burst even further. But what did she expect? He was half lion, and that half didn't want a woman by his side, not even the woman the *sapiya* had linked to him.

She didn't try to persuade him to let her spend the rest of the day with him. She knew it was pointless. Besides, how much begging could she do? Jenny needed to leave with her dignity intact.

On her next day off, she drove to Santa Barbara to see Matt. She needed to talk to someone, and her cousin was the logical choice.

So here she was, sitting in Matt's disgustingly messy apartment, with him waiting to hear what was on her mind. Only thing was, she couldn't be completely honest. Not that Matt would believe that Noah was a real shapeshifter anyway. But she wouldn't betray Noah's secret either way.

She embarked on the other subject that was consuming her. "Do you think that dreams carry messages?"

"Why? Did you have a weird dream?"

"No." At least that wasn't a lie. "I was just wondering how potent you think they are."

He grinned. "Wet dreams can be pretty potent."

"*Matt.*"

"Sorry." He laughed. "But hey, you're the one who's messing around with a guy who owns a sex club."

She knew exactly whom she was messing around with. "I wasn't referring to erotic dreams. Just the normal kind."

"Like falling and flying and things like that? Yeah, I think they carry messages about our emotions, thoughts, and impulses. Are you sure you didn't have a dream that's bugging you?"

She edged a little closer to the truth. "Someone had one about me."

"Someone who?"

"Noah. But I swear it wasn't about sex. It involved magic."

"Geez, is it any wonder? The stuff you told me about his club is freaky. People dressing up like mythical beings. It actually sounds kind of fun, though, and now I totally get why he went after you. A guy who's into mountain lions with the chick who rescues exotic cats." He made a thought-provoked expression. "If I was going to pretend to be part animal, what type do you think I'd be?"

She glanced at the crusty plates on the coffee table, left over from heaven only knew how many meals. "Maybe the pig variety?"

"Ha-ha. Pigs aren't even dirty animals. They wallow in the mud to keep cool."

"I know. I'm a zoologist, remember? I was just making a stupid joke."

He shrugged. "So why are you concerned about the dream Noah had? Did it involve scary magic?"

"It could have, I suppose. But he protected me from it."

"Then that sounds like a good message." Obviously Matt assumed Noah's protection had been part of the dream, not something after the fact.

"It *is* good." No matter how it came about. But the mystery of why the *sapiya* had drawn Jenny into it in the first place was weighing her down. To her, it didn't make sense if the end result was nothing more than an affair with Noah.

"You're really into this guy, aren't you?" Matt asked.

She nodded. She wasn't going to fib about that.

"Once you stop sleeping with him, you'll get over him."

If only it were that simple.

A moment later, her cell phone rang and she grabbed it out of her purse, hoping it was Noah, but the number on the screen was unfamiliar. She let the call go to voice mail.

But a little later, while Matt was in the bathroom, she checked the message and discovered it was Stanley Truxton, aka Noah's accountant, aka Coyote from the club.

And he wanted to talk to Jenny about Noah's dream.

Noah's phone rang. He answered it, and Coyote came on the line and said, "Guess who I'm meeting for dinner?"

Seriously? That was the reason for this call? Noah had better things to do with his time. "I couldn't care less."

"But this is someone I'm excited about."

"Fine, then tell me who it is."

"You're supposed to guess."

For cripe's sake. "I don't fucking know."

"Come on, play along. Think about it."

Noah took a moment to consider what type of person Coyote would be excited about dining with. A celebrity, probably. He was always clamoring after the stars and already had a fairly impressive roster of A-list clientele.

Off the top of his head, Noah recited the name of a spoiled young actress who loved to pose for the paparazzi.

"Nope," Coyote said.

He rattled off another party girl's name.

"Wrong again."

"Do I have the gender right?"

"Yes. But aside from her being blond and female, you're way off base."

So it wasn't young Hollywood. "You're getting together with Jean Harlow."

"Smart-ass. She died in 1937."

Noah smiled. "You should be dead by now, too."

Coyote laughed. "So should you."

"True. But Harlow was hot in her day."

"This woman is hot, too. But she's not a bombshell. She's much more innocent."

"An innocent actress? Does that even exist?"

"I never said she was an actress."

"Then just tell me who it is. I don't have all day to screw around playing guessing games with you."

"Okay, but you're not going to like it." A pause, then, "It's your latest lover. The lovely Ms. Jenny."

Noah snapped. "You little prick. What the hell are you up to?"

"I didn't have anything to do today, so I took the liberty of calling her. She was surprised that I knew what was going on. But apparently my timing is perfect because she's anxious to get my take on the dream, and I'm looking forward to sharing my 'Beauty and the Beast' thoughts with her."

"That's what this is about? That fairy-tale cock-and-bull?"

"I already told you that it's a perfectly lovely story."

Noah damned himself. Confiding in Coyote was a mistake he never intended to repeat. "I should fire you as my accountant and ban you from Aeonian."

"Oh, don't be so dramatic. You should be grateful that I'm giving you a heads-up."

"You're not telling me for my benefit. You're playing both ends of the field."

"Of course I am. Everything I do is for my own amusement. But somewhere in my trickster heart, you know that I love you. You're like a brother to me."

"The way Cain was a brother to Abel? Go fuck yourself."

The traitor chuckled. "I would if I could. I'm not big and handsome like you. I hardly ever get laid, even at that raunchy club of yours."

"Your half-assed sex life is the least of my concerns."

"Says the shifter who's bored with all of the pussy that's available to him. But that's why you seduced Jenny, isn't it? To combat the boredom? Then you go and have a powerful dream about her. Gosh, who knew it would be this exciting?"

A moment of nerve-grating silence passed.

Coyote spoke again. "Oh, and just in case you're wondering, I'm meeting her at a quaint little eatery in Santa Barbara. She suggested it, and it sounds fabulous."

"I wasn't wondering about the damned restaurant." But now that it had been mentioned, he envisioned Jenny at a candlelit table, listening to Coyote spin his yarn. Would she think it was ridiculous? Or would she hang on every word?

"I'd better go," the other man said, much too gleefully. "I don't want to be late."

Coyote hung up, and Noah cursed. The last thing he needed was Jenny getting storybook notions about him.

Eight

Jenny studied her dinner partner. He was an average-looking guy with short brown hair, narrow features, and conservative clothes. Although he fit the stereotype of an accountant, she'd met him at the club under the guise of Coyote, and that was how she'd come to think of him.

"Why did Noah tell you about his dream?" she asked.

"He needed someone to talk to, and I'm one of the few mortals who knows that he's a real shapeshifter."

Was Coyote mortal? With his thin lips and pointed nose, he actually resembled the animal he likened himself to, much in the way that Noah had natural catlike qualities, even in his human form.

He looked about, taking in the atmosphere. "This place is as quaint as you said it would be." He opened his menu. "I like Italian food. But I like everything. I'm not a fussy eater."

Jenny continued to study him. In the wild, coyotes were capable of adapting to different environments and often changed their breeding habits, diet, and social practices to go along with it.

"Any recommendations?" he asked.

"I normally get tortellini Alfredo."

"That sounds good. I'll order that, too. Do you want to share an appetizer? Let's see . . ." He scanned the selections. "How about calamari fritti?"

"Sorry, but squid always sounded a bit icky to me. But you can get it, if you want to."

"No, no. I'd rather share." He gazed at her from the top of his menu. "What about a nice, safe antipasto platter?"

She agreed and soon the waiter appeared and took their orders. Once the appetizer arrived, they nibbled on a variety of deli meats, cheeses, and vegetables.

"I told Noah that I was having dinner with you," Coyote said. "And now he's upset with me."

Jenny didn't know what to think. "Why did you tell him?"

"For the fun of it."

The salami she'd been eating hit her stomach like a rock. "This isn't a game to me."

"I know." He skewered an olive. "Now, why don't we get down

to business, and I'll tell you my theory. You're dying to hear it, aren't you?"

"Dying" wasn't the word she would have chosen, at least not while she was seated across from a man who might be a real coyote. Then again, she'd been sleeping with a lion shapeshifter, and that was far more dangerous.

He said, "Since the *sapiya* referred to Noah as a beast, I think they want you to try to save him."

"Save him?"

"In a 'Beauty and the Beast' kind of way. Are you familiar with that story?"

"I know it's a fairy tale and that Disney made a movie of it. But I've never seen it."

"Actually, the original author is unknown, but the first published version was in the eighteenth century. It's been rewritten many times since." Coyote leaned forward. "Would you like me to highlight my favorite rendition for you?"

Unable to contain her curiosity, she nodded.

He started with, "Belle, or Beauty as she has come to be known, is a dear girl, beautiful and pure of heart. She has two equally beautiful sisters, but they are selfish and never satisfied." He popped another olive into his mouth. "Their father is a merchant who lost his wealth, but he is pursuing a means to regain his assets. Before he embarks on a trip, the older daughters insist that he bring back costly gifts. All Belle wants is the safe return of her father, but she doesn't want to offend her sisters by not asking for anything, so she requests a rose."

Jenny remained glued to her seat, foolishly seeing herself as Belle.

Coyote continued, "The merchant is unable to regain his wealth and on his way home, he becomes lost in a cold, dark forest. He finds shelter in a castle, where a feast awaits him. He eats the food, drinks the wine, and falls asleep by the fire, but he doesn't meet the owner of the castle."

"Is it Beast?"

"Yes, but let's not get ahead of ourselves."

"Sorry; go ahead."

"The next morning, the merchant leaves the interior of the castle and wanders the grounds. On his way out, he notices a rose garden. Recalling that Belle wants a rose, he picks the prettiest one he can find. Then he is approached by a horrid beast."

Jenny envisioned Noah, only he wasn't horrid, of course. But he was still a sight to behold.

"Beast claims that the merchant has just taken his most prized possession and must die for his crime. He locks the merchant in the castle, intending to kill him."

The waiter arrived with their entrees and interrupted the story. Once the server was gone, Coyote didn't resume talking. He tasted his tortellini first.

Finally he said, "When Beauty hears that her father has been imprisoned and is awaiting death, she goes to the castle and offers herself as his replacement. Beast agrees to the arrangement and releases the merchant."

Jenny ate a bite of her meal. "Is Beauty frightened when she first sees Beast?"

"Oh, yes. Terribly so. She trembles when she speaks to him."

"And what does he think of her?"

"He is impressed that she is willing to die for her father's crime. As the days pass, Beauty wonders when Beast is going to kill her and worries about the manner in which it will happen. But he treats her kindly instead. They dine together each night, and although she still finds him frightening to look at, she is pleased by his goodness."

"Noah is much wilder than Beast. He would've seduced Beauty by now."

"I suspect that Beast wanted to, but it wouldn't have been seemly then."

"What happens next?"

"Beast asks Beauty to marry him. This shocks her, and she refuses. But he doesn't give up. He proposes every day, hoping that she will be become his bride."

"But she never agrees?"

"No, but she vows that she will never leave him altogether. Still, she asks if she can visit her family and promises to return in a week. Beasts allows her to go and tells her that he will die of a broken heart if she doesn't come back."

Entranced, Jenny waited to see the outcome.

"Beauty goes home, but she gets trapped by her sisters and isn't able to keep her promise to Beast. When she finally returns to the castle, she finds him unconscious and near death. She throws herself across his body and listens to the faint beat of his heart. Knowing that she loves him, she begs him to live so they can be married. As soon as she says this, the castle lights up and Beast turns into a handsome prince."

Like the silly female she was fast becoming, Jenny visualized the sparkling scene in her mind. "How did he become a beast in the first place?"

"He was cursed."

"Do you think the woman who turned Noah was cursed? Do you think that's how she became a shifter?"

"I don't know, but it would be interesting to find out."

"If she was cursed and the spell could be broken, then Noah would probably go back to normal, too."

"Like Beast?" Coyote smiled. "Do you want me to look into it? To try to find out who she was?"

"Will you actually do that or are you tricking me?"

"I'll do it, but I'm not going to keep it a secret from Noah. It would be more fun to bring him into the loop."

Jenny wasn't thinking about fun. She was thinking about saving Noah and whether it was actually possible. "It's going to make him angry."

"He'll just have to learn to deal with it." Coyote removed his cell phone. "I'm going to tell him right now."

This soon? "No, don't—"

Too late. He made the call.

Afterward, he grinned. "He's pissed, all right. Now let's finish our dinner."

Jenny could barely eat, but Coyote savored every morsel of his meal and topped it off with spumoni. She sat idly by while he spooned into his ice cream and chatted about inconsequential things.

They finally parted ways, and by the time her headlights shined on the narrow path that led to her house, her mind was in a tizzy. Dealing with Noah wasn't going to be easy.

She walked toward her porch, then started.

There he sat, glaring up at her. He must have headed right to her place after Coyote called him. He was in his human form, but that didn't make him any less menacing.

He stood up. "So you're going to try to find a way to save me?"

She slowed her steps. "Coyote offered."

"This is a big fucking game to him."

"Yes, but it's not a game to me."

"I don't want to be saved."

"Maybe deep down you do. Maybe you're more like Beast than you're willing to admit."

"That story is a load of crap."

"The *sapiya* called you a beast." She took a chance and inched closer to him. "So maybe they want me to be like Beauty."

His glare got deeper. "Why? So we'll fall stupidly in love? Get real, Jenny."

His admonishment hit her like a fist, packing a big, scary wallop. "I never said that's where this was leading."

"Then what's your agenda? Why save me if you're not interested in being with me?"

"I'm just exploring the possibility of what the *sapiya* wants."

"Why would you do that unless you thought there was a future in it?"

"All right, so it crossed my mind that maybe it's supposed to be more than an affair. But I never consciously used the word 'love.'"

"And you'd better not, either."

The scary wallop came back. Loving him would be a disaster, especially if making him mortal *wasn't* possible. But the fact that she was already getting attached only managed to exacerbate her fears, as well as her anger.

She snapped at him. "Don't tell me what I'm supposed to do or how I'm allowed to feel."

He snapped right back. "I should whisk your stubborn little ass off to a castle and show you what it's like to be locked up with a real beast."

"As if you would."

"I have enough money to pull it off."

She challenged him. "Then do it, Noah. Flaunt your wealth and show me how beastly you can be."

"Fine. You want a goddamn fairy tale, I'll give you one. But it's going to be warped." He snatched her keys and unlocked the front door.

They went inside, and he made a beeline for her computer. He started it up, got online, and searched for "Castles for rent in California."

Was there such a thing? Jenny wondered.

Sure enough, there was. Noah found one in a wooded area that suited him, and she stood over his shoulder and read the information on the screen. With more than a hundred rooms, the three-story structure had been built for weddings, special events, and private getaways.

He checked the website and rattled off upcoming dates that were available. They chose a day that fit their schedules, and he made a reservation.

She gazed at the pictures of the enormous castle. It was magnificent, but overwhelming, too. "Just how warped is this adventure going to be?"

"Getting cold feet?"

"I was just wondering what you had in mind."

"You'll find out when the times comes." He shut down her computer. "Be prepared to play Beauty's part." He shifted into cat form and trailed a claw along her blouse, making a deliberate cut in the sleeve. "Without the happily ever after."

On the day of the outing, Jenny was chauffeured to the location by the same driver who'd been taking her back and forth to the club. She had no idea if Noah was already at the castle or would be arriving later, but as the town car approached the building, butterflies the size of helicopters erupted in her stomach.

Surrounded by towering redwoods, the castle was even more imposing than it had been in pictures.

The driver parked and opened Jenny's door. She got out and stood beside him.

"What happens now?" she asked.

He removed her bags from the trunk. "I've been instructed to take you to your suite."

They went inside, and the entrance with its cathedral ceilings, gilded archways, and sweeping staircase left her awestruck.

He bypassed the stairs and led her to the east wing. They stopped at a lavish door with a sign on it that read, "Beauty."

The suite offered a sitting room, a bedroom, and a connecting bath, all of it fit for a princess.

After a moment of silence, he directed her to a gold-leafed armoire in the bedroom. Upon opening it, he said, "Each of these is in your size."

She stared at the elaborate gowns. Jenny didn't know much about old-style clothes, but she assumed they were similar to fashions from the eighteenth century, when "Beauty and the Beast" had first appeared in print.

"A selection of shoes and undergarments has been provided, as well," he said.

For now, it seemed wonderfully romantic, but she suspected that was part of Noah's "warped" plan.

The driver spoke again. "After I depart, you're supposed to don the gown of your choice and fix your hair and makeup." He gestured to a mirrored vanity table. "There are jeweled combs and ribbons in the drawer if you'd like to use an ornament for your coiffure."

"What am I supposed to do after I'm ready?"

"Wander the castle and search for your host."

She widened her eyes. "By myself?"

He nodded.

"But there are over a hundred rooms in this place."

"I'm sorry, miss. But I can't alter what's been required of you." With that, he left, closing the door behind him.

Trapped inside the demented fairy tale Noah had created, Jenny went through the armoire and chose a blue gown with a velvet-trimmed bodice. She was nervous, but strangely aroused, too, especially when she discovered that the undergarments were a corset and petticoat. Nothing had been provided to serve as panties, so she assumed that she was supposed to go bare underneath.

Before she got dressed, she sat at the vanity to do her hair. Because she wasn't skilled in that regard, she redid it several times, trying to get it right. Finally she managed to pin it up in a softly creative way. She added a jeweled comb to one side.

Her makeup required a light touch-up, so she applied a bit of blush and the pink lipstick she'd become accustomed to wearing.

Climbing into the clothing was a chore. She wasn't used to

tiny hooks and poufy fabrics, but at least everything fastened in front.

Jenny gazed at her reflection in a full-length mirror. It had taken almost two hours to complete the look, but this was the prettiest she'd ever been. She'd never felt so ladylike.

She noticed an antique perfume bottle on the vanity and tested the fragrance. It was sweet and genteel. She sprayed a bit of it on her neck and wrists.

She exited her suite and stood in the hallway, unsure of which direction to go.

Beauty didn't have a clue how to find Beast.

Nine

What should she do first? Check the wing she was in? Head over to the other side of the castle? Or go upstairs?

She chose the stairs and took them to the second floor. Roaming the hallway, she tried every door and discovered all of the rooms were locked.

The third floor proved more complicated, as it was a maze of hallways and connecting corridors. But again, every door was locked.

What if Noah wasn't even here? What if she was all alone in this place? No, she told herself. That wouldn't make sense. Whatever he had in store, it involved the two of them.

Jenny returned to the lower level and came upon a door with a sign that read, "Beast."

Her pulse pounded in her ears. This was it. She'd found him.

Anxious, she turned the doorknob and crossed the threshold, which opened into a parlor, similar to the sitting room in her suite, only bigger and with masculine furnishings.

Since the parlor and kitchenette were empty, she proceeded to the bedroom, which was also vacant of Noah's presence. So was the adjoining bathroom.

Now what?

Befuddled, Jenny exited Beast's suite and continued her quest, heading for yet another wing.

On and on she went, like a storybook heroine in distress. The more time that passed, the more nervous she got. Then an eerie thought crossed her mind. Was Noah watching her? Had he set up spy equipment to track her throughout the castle?

Soon she found another door, actually a set of double doors, which were labeled, "Ballroom."

Was this her final destination?

She tried the handles, but they wouldn't open. Damn it. How was she supposed to find him if he was one step ahead of her the entire time?

Jenny was tempted to return to her room and pout, but that would make her look weak. No way was she going to give him that kind of victory.

A few minutes later, she saw a glass door with a sign that read, "Rose Garden." She tried the door and it opened. But since the path wasn't lit and dusk had long since fallen, she hesitated. Surely, he didn't expect her to go stumbling outside in the dark.

No, apparently he didn't. Because as she stood there, gazing out at the night, a sprinkling of lights appeared. Now she knew for sure that he was watching her.

Would Beast appear among the flowers, like he did in the story when he'd caught the merchant plucking a rose for Beauty?

Cautious, Jenny ventured onto the path, looking to and fro. Color bloomed all around her, but there was no sign of Noah. At the end of the stone walkway was a greenhouse.

She approached the building, which had a sign on the door with instructions: "Wait here."

For the heck of it, she tried the handle. It was locked. Clearly, she was meant to wait outside. She prayed the lights didn't go off.

Luckily, they stayed on, and much to her surprise, the door opened and out walked her driver.

"Hello, miss," he said.

She didn't chide him for duping her. He was, after all, Noah's loyal employee. Funny, too, because she didn't even know his name, but now didn't seem like the time to ask.

"Good evening." She tried to reply the way Beauty would. "As you can see, I'm still searching for my host."

"He requests your presence in the ballroom."

"Are you here to escort me?"

"Sorry, no. I'm just the messenger." He gestured for her to take the path from whence she'd come.

Picking up her skirts, she returned to the interior of the castle.

She'd agreed to this twisted fairy tale. It wasn't as if she hadn't been forewarned.

Would the ballroom doors be unlocked this time? Or was this another wild-goose chase? She tried the handles, and thankfully, they worked.

Granting herself entrance, she marveled at the enchantment. Hundreds of white votives burned throughout the grand room, which was already glorified with a jewel-toned floor and stained-glass windows. In the center of it all, a crystal chandelier shined over a lone dining table.

The table was set for two, and on one of the chairs was a delicate red rose. Clearly that was Beauty's seat. But where was Beast?

She lifted the flower and stroked its velvet-soft petals. Since the stem was about the right length to fit comfortably into her bodice, she tucked the rose between her breasts.

As soon as it was secure, footsteps sounded behind her, creating a ghostly sound.

She turned and saw Noah, who'd just entered the room, and her heart echoed the tap, tap, tap of his feet.

Attired in a regal suit that she assumed was from the same era as her dress, he actually looked like a prince turned beast. His tawny-streaked hair was fastened into a ponytail. Or was it called a queue in those days? Whatever the terminology, it left the angles of his face unframed, making his shapeshifter features more pronounced.

Jenny's voice quavered. "I looked everywhere for you."

"I'm aware of how diligently you searched."

"I suspected that you were tracking me."

"I would've sent someone to retrieve you if you'd gotten lost. I wouldn't have allowed you to wander the halls the entire night." He angled his head. "Although I imagine it was starting to feel like forever to you."

Was he mocking her? Reminding her that he intended to live for an eternity, in spite of her interest in saving him?

She responded, "Forever is a long time. Too long, I think."

He glanced at the rose between her breasts. "Not if it's what someone has become accustomed to."

She fought a breath of desire. "Are we sparring already?"

"So it seems." He gestured to her place setting. "Shall we dine?"

Jenny nodded. She was famished: for food, for him, for their strange evening to progress.

He scooted in her chair, then sat across from her and said, "We'll be having a five-course meal, prepared by a catering service that works regularly at castle events. I just need to let them know that my dinner companion has arrived." He removed his cell phone from his jacket and punched out a text.

"They've been waiting in the kitchen all this time?"

"They knew when I hired them that this was a private masquerade." He put his phone back. "Of course, they don't have a clue that my costume is real."

She spread her napkin across her lap. The caterers didn't know, but she certainly did.

He reached for a bottle of cabernet sauvignon that was already on the table and poured it into their glasses. "This is from the year you were born."

She took a sip. "To reinforce how fragile my mortality is?"

"Actually it's just a nice vintage. But if you want to equate it with your fragility, who am I to argue?" He tasted his wine and offered her a slice of bread. It, too, was already on the table. "You look dazzling, by the way. I like that you chose the blue dress. It matches your eyes."

She thanked him for the bread and the compliment. "All of the gowns were beautiful, but this was my favorite. I never imagined myself in anything so glamorous."

"Tonight you're Beauty locked in Beast's castle." Noah glanced around. "It's impressive, isn't it?"

"Extremely." She studied him from beneath the chandelier. He was as impressive as the surroundings.

He gazed at her, too, and while they continued to look at each other, a tuxedoed waiter entered the ballroom with shrimp cocktail as their first course.

After he departed, they ate silently.

The next course was a wild greens salad, and the third was lemon sorbet to cleanse their palates.

A short while later, the main entrée arrived: beef tenderloin stuffed with mushrooms, and baby red potatoes seasoned with rosemary and carved into hearts.

Jenny waited until the waiter was gone before she said, "Heart-shaped potatoes?"

"It wasn't my idea."

"But you approved the menu ahead of time, didn't you?"

"It seemed to fit with the fairy-tale setting." He sliced into one of the potatoes in question, breaking it in half. "Besides, mountain lions eat the hearts from their prey. You provided me with that information yourself."

She pretended to shrug off his comment, even if it made her uncomfortable. She didn't want to think about him devouring her heart, not literally or figuratively, and especially not after he'd warned her not to fall in love with him.

"You know what I just realized?" He topped off her wine. "You know more about me than I know about you."

"How do you figure?"

"I told you about my family history, but you haven't told me about yours."

"You know about my grandfather."

"Yes, but what about your parents? Who are they?"

"I never met my father. He left before I was born." She cut into her tenderloin, but she didn't take a bite. "My mother died when I was five, so I barely knew her, either. She had a brain aneurysm. It happened really suddenly. We were already living with my grandfather, so I stayed there and he raised me."

He frowned. "Maybe I should be trying to save you. Your story sounds more tragic than mine."

"I don't think so. I had a good life with Grandpa." She considered the circumstances. "And now I'm running the rescue he founded. The place I would've lost if it hadn't been for you and your money. In that sense, you already did save me."

"For a sexual price," he reminded her.

She ate the beef she'd gently knifed. "You still did it."

"Only because I'm a rich beast who wanted to fuck you. Do you know how I amassed my fortune?"

She shook her head. She'd never thought to inquire.

"By investing in gold."

"That was a smart thing to do."

"Being immortal has its perks. Is it any wonder I intend to stay this way?"

She struggled to level the playing field. "It's a long time to be alone, Noah."

"So we're back to *forever* and how long it is?"

Yes, they were back to that. "How have you managed to fit into society for all this time? Don't the people you're around start to notice that you don't age?"

"I don't stay in one place long enough for them to notice. I move. I change my identity. I go into seclusion and come back when enough time has passed."

"Is Aeonian the first business you've ever owned?"

He nodded. "Other supernaturals have run clubs before. Speakeasies, discos, whatever was in vogue. But my club is the first one where we could hide in plain sight. Eventually I'll have to sell it, though, and move on. Or close it down or whatever. Eventually it will be time to disappear again."

She couldn't seem to stop herself from asking, "How would you have lived out your life if you hadn't been attacked and could've gone back to Indian Territory? Do you think you would've gotten married and had a family of your own?"

"That's a pointless question."

"I think it's relevant."

"To what? Me being mortal again? That isn't going to happen, and what I would've done all those years ago has no bearing on my existence now." He motioned to her food. "Why haven't you touched your potatoes?"

The quick change of topic rattled her. "I haven't gotten around to them yet."

"I thought maybe you didn't want to destroy them." He made her aware of his plate, where they were all chopped up. "The way I did."

She refused to cringe at the hearts he'd mangled. She even went ahead and stabbed one of hers. Noah watched her, as if he were expecting it to bleed.

Before things got too awkward, she summoned her composure. "What are the caterers going to serve for dessert?"

"Chocolate torte wrapped in chocolate ribbons. It's their specialty."

"That sounds wonderful."

"Glad you think so. Because afterward, we're going to go to my suite and you're going to get on your knees for me." He tipped his glass to her. "Does that sound wonderful, too?"

She went warm and instantly wet. Chocolate with an oral sex chaser. Something sweet. Something salty. "Will I be removing my dress before I do it?"

He nodded.

"What about my undergarments?"

"You'll be keeping those on."

She envisioned herself in corset and petticoat, crawling on the floor between his legs. "Are you going to give me instructions?"

"Yes, I am. But you know what's even better than that? I have a camera in my room so I can record it, and when we're done, we can watch it."

Her breath rushed out, nearly dislodging the bodice-trapped rose. He went back to his meal, and she sat there, her mind in a whir.

Beauty was going to make a sex tape with Beast.

After dessert, Noah's eagerness mounted. He took Jenny to his suite, and now she stood beside the bed in her silk-and-velvet dress, waiting for him to set up the camera equipment and tell her what to do.

Once it was operable and the video was running, he said, "Take off your dress."

She did as she was told. First she removed the flower, then fumbled with the tiny hooks on the bodice. He wasn't about to rush her. Part of the allure was her inexperience, and the cumbersome garment wasn't helping. Neither was her awareness of the camera.

It took a while, but she stepped out of the gown. She looked around for somewhere to put it, then placed it on the bed. He wouldn't have cared if she'd left it on the floor. But the fact that she'd taken such special care of it only heightened the moment. Her underwear wasn't going to receive the same kind of gentle treatment, at least not by him. Eventually he intended to claw them off her.

"Should I get on my knees now?"

"Not yet." He wanted more time to touch her. He traced the lines of the corset. "I used to be fascinated by these because Seminole women didn't wear them. The first one I saw was on a white woman. She was blond, like you." He took the comb out of her hair and tossed it aside.

"Who was she?"

"A whore."

"You slept with prostitutes?"

"They were the only white women willing to be with me then."

"I would've been with you."

They gazed at each other for a soundless moment. Confused by the way she was making him feel, he said, "For the record, I was planning on getting married when I was mortal."

Her voice jumped. "You were? To who?"

"No one in particular. I just assumed I'd have a wife someday."

"My grandpa always told me that I'd have a husband someday. Someone who shares my love of big cats."

"As opposed to someone who's half-cat?"

"That isn't what I meant. Besides, you told me I'm not allowed to care about you."

"But that's not going to stop you from trying to save me, is it?"

"I can't help it. It just feels like it's something I should do."

Noah looked into her eyes. By now she seemed unaware of the camera and completely focused on him. If they'd hailed from the same era, would he have chosen her for his bride?

Troubled by the thought, he went back to talking about the whore. "The blonde in the corset gave me my first blow job."

"What if I don't please you the way she did?"

"You'll be better than she was." Without thinking, he leaned in to kiss her, and their tongues met and mated. She tasted like chocolate, but he supposed that he did, too.

Half-hard and ready for more, he ended the kiss. "You can get on your knees now."

She lowered herself to the floor, the petticoat making a half-moon behind her. The flouncy garment was a profusion of lace and ribbons, the exact opposite of his masculine attire.

He ditched his jacket and tie, unbuttoned his shirt, and opened his pants. "I changed my mind about giving you instructions. I'm going to let you figure it out on your own."

"But I'm not good at it. I need you to guide me through it. Or else I won't be better at it than she was."

"Who told you that you weren't good?"

"No one. I just know that I'm not."

"You're going to do just fine." Noah freed his cock and moved closer to her face.

She looked up at him. "Can I use my hands first? Can I do that for a while?"

"You can do whatever comes natural."

She explored him gently, stroking him from shaft to tip. Her touch was tentative, and it aroused him beyond reason. None of the whores had ever handled him this way, and neither did the groupies at the club. He'd forgotten what it was like to be with a woman whose sexual confidence wavered. When she cupped his balls, he sucked in his breath.

Sweet sin. Could she be any more perfect?

She moistened her lips and kissed each testicle. She rubbed her cheek against his cock, too, teasing him with the softness of her skin. Everything she did was an aphrodisiac.

Tonight, she'd stepped out of the pages of a fairy tale, and so had he. Beauty and the Beast. She had her instincts, and he had his. He was looking forward to ripping her corset and petticoat to shreds before the night was through.

He delved into her upswept hair, unearthing bobby pins. Waves tumbled and fell, framing her face. She was still nuzzling his cock, and the camera was still rolling, capturing every nuance.

While she tongued the tip of him, Noah wanted to end the

madness and shove his cock down her throat. But he reined himself back.

She finally wrapped her mouth around him, and it was the best fucking feeling in the world.

All he could think about was coming.

She made naughty little sounds, and he continued to ravage her hair, making a glorious mess out of it.

As she sucked, she gripped the base of his shaft. Crazy with need, he rocked forward, thrusting deeper. She wasn't able to swallow him all the way, but she seemed to be doing her best, and it was plenty good.

More than good.

Noah couldn't take his eyes off her, but she wasn't looking at him. She had her eyes closed, concentrating on his pleasure.

Wicked innocence at its finest.

He fought for control, but she was his undoing, his lust, his hunger. Pressure built in his loins, and adrenaline skyrocketed through his veins.

With a pounding heart, he tugged viciously on her hair and growled, alerting her that he was going to come.

Her eyes shot open, and they stared at each other. In the next dirty-sweet instant, she tipped back her head so he could watch himself spill into her mouth

Ending it with a hot-blooded bang.

Ten

After Noah fastened his pants and turned off the camera, Jenny got up off her knees, righting her petticoat.

He went over to the wet bar and returned with a drink for her. "It's ginger ale."

"Thank you." She sipped the soda.

"Do you want to watch the video?"

"Now?" She hadn't forgotten that they'd been making a sex tape, but now that it was over, she needed a moment to process what she'd done.

"Better now than later. Because later I plan on getting a second wind and fucking you until you scream."

Her heart lurched beneath her corset. "You're not going to record that, too, are you?"

"I think one dirty tape is enough. Don't you?"

She nodded. More than enough.

While she finished the ginger ale, he sat at a rolltop desk and transferred the file from his camera onto his laptop. He then copied it onto a CD.

He turned to face her. "Do you know why I chose this suite for Beast's room?"

She shook her head.

"Because of the iron posts on the bed. They're perfect for bondage."

Her heart lurched again. Her dress was still draped across the bed. To keep herself busy, she hung it in the closet. "Are you going to tie me up while you're making me scream?"

"Yes, I am. But first let's watch the show."

He put the CD in the built-in player on the TV, and Jenny battled a wave of self-consciousness. "Can't we watch it on your laptop instead?"

"This is better. Bigger."

Too big, she thought. The screen was probably fifty inches.

He put the remote on the nightstand and propped the pillows on the bed. "Should I make some popcorn?"

Was he kidding? She couldn't be sure. Just in case he was serious, she said, "I'm still full from dinner."

"You're probably still full from what I gave you, too. Cripes, that was amazing." He got in bed and patted the space next to him. "And now we can see it in high definition."

She crawled in beside him, and he hit the Play button. The video started with Jenny lifting the rose from her bodice and awkwardly removing her gown.

"You look beautiful up there," Noah said. He glanced over. "You still do."

She scooted closer to him, and he reached for her hand and held it. They were actually cuddling in bed. Granted, there was a sex tape involved, but it was still a cozy way to be.

The video continued: Noah examining her corset while he talked about his first blow job. Then, all too soon, the marriage discussion arose, and on the screen, Jenny and Noah were gazing at each other with emotion in their eyes.

"This is the boring part," he said.

It was far from boring, but she withheld her opinion. If she expressed how romantic she thought it was, she feared it would shatter their current closeness. He was still holding her hand.

They kept watching, and when they kissed in the video, she nearly sighed. They made an engaging couple: an inexperienced blonde in old-fashioned underwear and a passionate beast.

"Now we're getting somewhere," he said.

There they were, as big as life, Jenny on her knees, and Noah pulling his cock out of his pants.

Oh, goodness. She got concerned. "This better not show up on the Internet."

"I'd never put it out there."

"But someone else might. What if your camera gets lost or

stolen? Or a curious cleaning lady comes across the CD in your apartment?" She wouldn't put it past a groupie, either, but she didn't want to mention him bringing other women home.

"Don't worry. I'll erase it from my camera and destroy the disc after we're done watching it." He angled his head. "Damn, look how sweet you are, stroking me with your hands."

Because she couldn't quite shake the other women from her mind, she dared to ask, "Was I better than the whore?"

"God, yes. You were better than anyone."

Her pussy reacted to his praise, all aflutter beneath the girly petticoat.

He lifted their joined hands and motioned to the TV. "Check you out. Kissing my balls and nuzzling my dick like a little kitten. Damn, this is turning me on. Ah, there. You went for it. My cock between your lips. This is so hot."

Burning hot.

The memory pulsed like fire. In the video, Noah was destroying her coiffure.

He continued to comment. "I love how your hair was tumbling around your face. It felt so soft and silky between my fingers, so tangled and pretty."

It remained just as messy. She hadn't tried to smooth it, nor did she intend to. Would he tug on it later? Would that be part of the bondage?

On camera, Jenny's eyes were closed, and in real time, her

blood hummed, streaming through her veins. "This is making me crazy."

"How crazy?"

"I want you to tie me up and fuck me."

"Not yet."

"Then I want to touch myself. I want to lift my petticoat and stroke my clit."

"That's naughty, sweet girl. But you need to behave. I want you focused until the end. I want you to see how sexy it was when you swallowed all that milky-white come."

She squeezed her thighs together. Not fair. He was talking dirty while her other self was gripping the base of his shaft and sucking deep.

"What did it feel like to have my cock in your mouth?" he asked.

She relived the sensation. "It was warm and hard and heavy, and when I glided my tongue over it, I felt every ridge and flare."

He turned the volume up, intensifying the oral sounds: the wetness of her mouth, the friction of his skin.

The visual seemed to heighten, too: the bobbing of her head, the rocking motion of his hips.

It was all there, in living, blasting color.

"It's about to happen," he said. "This is where you open your eyes, and I spill into you. Watch, Jenny, watch."

She was, and it was driving her mad.

A second later, TV Noah growled, and TV Jenny tossed back her head and drank from him.

The final frame went dark. He shut it off, and silence engulfed the room. Searing with need, she waited.

Tick . . . tick . . . tick . . .

She glanced at his fly. It bulged at the seams.

Cock . . . cock . . . cock . . .

He walked over to the closet and came back with four pieces of silky rope. It was rougher than the flowing ties she'd expected, but still soft enough not to chafe her delicate skin.

Or so she assumed.

"Spread eagle," he told her. "Then draw your knees up and plant your feet flat on the mattress."

She got into the required position, and since her underwear remained in place, it created a twisted sense of modesty. Her legs were open, but she wasn't exposed.

He secured her wrists and ankles to the bedposts. The rope didn't hurt, but the knots were expertly bound, and she realized that he could do whatever he wanted, and she was helpless to stop him. But the biggest danger was how desperately she thrived on the fear.

He crawled into bed and bared his claws. Jenny actually gulped. "What are you going to do with those?"

"Just hold still. Very, very still."

She didn't move a muscle, not even an involuntary twitch.

Using one pointed tip like a knife, he sliced the ties on the front of her corset. The stiff fabric parted, slowly, like cracked armor, and her breasts popped out. The air in her lungs rushed out, too.

"There," he said. "The start of Beauty's unveiling."

She tried to imagine how she looked, strapped to a castle bed, with her corset deliberately ruined, but she couldn't quite fathom it.

"Do you want to see yourself?" he asked, as if he'd caught wind of her curiosity. "I can show you." He gestured to the other side of the room, making her aware of a tall mirror encased in a wood frame.

The freestanding unit was on casters. As he rolled it over to the foot of the bed, it bumped across the polished stone floor.

"It's called a cheval mirror," he told her. "This one is from the same era as our fairy tale." He angled it so her reflection encompassed the glass. "What do you think?"

She didn't know what to say. Between her blow-job-swollen lips, disheveled hair, bared breasts, and bondage restraints, she looked like an eighteenth-century sacrifice. It was only a matter of time before he lifted her petticoat and had his way with her.

"Cat got your tongue?" he asked.

A trickle of moisture escaped from between her thighs. His little joke enhanced the thrill.

She replied, "He isn't a cat. He's a shapeshifter."

Noah sat beside her on the bed, putting his half-feline reflection in the mirror. He looked poised and polished, but hungry and invasive, too. "So he is."

He climbed on top of her, and the weight of male muscle

taunted her senses. If she'd had use of her arms, she would've flung them around his neck.

He lowered his head and took one of her nipples into his mouth, grazing the pink bud with his teeth before clamping his lips around it. He shifted to the other breast, repeating the rough foreplay and alternating back and forth.

She moaned, and he purred his enjoyment, the erotic rumble vibrating between their bodies. Fanning his hands on either side of her, he attacked the quilt with his claws, and the harder he sucked, the deeper the cuts got.

"They're going to make you pay to replace that," she said.

He lifted his head. "Are you scolding me?"

"No, I was just—"

"Trying to hurry me along?"

She nodded. The ache in her nipples was zinging straight to her pussy. "I want you to fuck me, like you promised."

He flashed his signature smile, lethal and sharp. "It's going to get worse before it gets better."

No doubt about that. He descended on her breasts again and the ache was almost too much to bear. Pleasure mingled with pain. The pull of his mouth got stronger and stronger.

He resumed his assault on the bed, and by the time he stopped, her nipples were red and raw, and the mattress itself had been used like a scratching post.

Dazed, she kept quiet, especially since he was reaching for her petticoat. Finally, he was going to lift it. Finally—

Riiiip.

He clawed the ruffled hem and pulled it apart with his hands, shredding the lace and tearing the garment in two. Jenny lay there, bound to a slashed-up bed, with her undergarments tattered and her heart racing. Completing the job, he tugged the corset and shorn petticoat out from under her and discarded them onto the floor.

"Do you still want me to fuck you?" he asked.

She nodded shakily, anxious for him to remove the remainder of his clothes and thrust into her. But he chose another form of wicked fun.

He untied her right hand and said, "Get yourself ready for me. Do it in front of the mirror." He sat beside her once more. "So we both can watch."

Her cheeks went hot. She'd wanted to stroke her clit earlier, but she hadn't envisioned anything quite like this. "I'm already ready." Surely he saw that she was glistening in her own juices.

"Do it anyway."

Jenny gazed at the sexually haunted woman in the glass. She moved her hand down, pressing her fingers against her clit.

"That's right," he said. "Rub it nice and slow."

She followed his command. She lifted her hips and tightened her rear, too, since that was how she normally pleasured herself in bed, but it was a dizzying sensation with her legs tied open.

"Now put your fingers inside and show me how sticky you are."

A knot of desire pulsed at her navel. She went deep into the walls of her vagina and produced the moisture.

He played yet another game. "Smear it on your lips and lick it off."

She tasted her own juice, and the tangy flavor burst on her tongue.

His eyes darkened and his nostrils flared. "I want some," he ground out, before he put his face between her legs and made her *seriously* wet.

Mouth-to-pussy wet. Man-tormenting-woman wet.

Jenny moaned, and he retracted his claws and spread her inner folds with greedy fingers, opening her all the way.

She looked in the mirror and tunneled her free hand through his hair, releasing the ponytail at his nape. The tawny-streaked strands shimmered in the antique glass, as bright as lunar-kissed gold.

At that magical moment, he seemed like a cursed prince, and she seemed like the maiden who was destined to save him.

His voice winged across her skin. "What letter of the alphabet do you think this is?" He made a motion with his tongue, writing something on her labia.

"I don't know." All she knew was how amazing it felt.

He licked out another letter, then another. He stopped after the fourth one. "Still can't tell?"

"I can't concentrate." Her mind was seductively jumbled.

"It was my name."

He repeated the process, and now that she knew what it was, she recognized every sizzling stroke: N-O-A-H.

She said, "I'm going to keep the rose you gave me."

"Keep it where?"

"Pressed between the pages of a book." Wasn't that what smitten girls did with special flowers?

He put a different spin on it. "I should buy you a dirty book to use."

"Whatever you want." She pitched her pelvis toward him, trying to get closer. He was swirling her clit, around and around. "Do your name there."

"Like this?"

"Yes." Just like that. Beast almighty. The next time she put her mouth on him, she was going to spell out her name, too, letter by wet letter, all the way across his big, hard cock.

"Again?" he asked.

She gasped out an unintelligible response. An orgasm bubbled beneath his touch, lifting her higher and higher.

Closing her fingers, she pulled on his hair. She'd imagined him tugging on hers as part of the bondage, but she was doing it to him.

She watched in the mirror, and with his mouth fused to her cunt, she let herself go. The climax hit in undulating waves, her ass taut, her back bowed.

No time to recover. Blocking the cheval, he sat up and stripped off his clothes, filling her vision with his fully erect penis.

He pounced, slamming between her legs and thrusting all the way inside. She tried to dig her nails into his back, but he grabbed her wrist and retied it to the bedpost.

No free hand. No freedom at all. He was the king of the castle, and she was his prisoner. The thrill of danger returned, pulsing deep and fierce within her core. The joining of aroused flesh created a slapping sound. The rise and fall of his chest crushed her breasts, renewing the ache in her sucked-sore nipples.

Boom. Boom. Boom.

Her heart drummed against his, and she panicked about falling in love with him. That it was truly happening.

Now? Like this? The bonds grew tighter as he moved. Fighting her feelings for him, she squeezed her eyes shut.

"Look at me," he demanded.

She opened her eyes, and his primal gaze burned straight into hers. In the next instant, he captured her mouth, and while their tongues sparred, he increased the pace.

A brutal rhythm with an immortal man.

A supernatural being.

The voracious kiss ended, but the feral fucking continued.

Her pussy swelled and contracted, every nerve ending welcoming the hard, thick length of his cock. She thrashed, caught in a fireball of pleasure, wanting it to stop, wanting it to last a lifetime. Beads of sweat broke out on her forehead, dampening her hairline. He was sweating, too, his skin clammy.

Her legs had gone numb, but she didn't care. She was on the verge of a volcanic orgasm. The pressure built, threatening to explode.

She gasped and jerked, twisting and pulling at the restraints. He didn't attempt to keep her still.

Jenny cried out when she came, and then Noah came, too, drenching her in well-aimed shots of semen.

The convulsions ceased. Their breathing slowed. He dropped down and purred softly against her neck. She reciprocated, issuing a spent sigh.

He lifted his rangy body, sitting up to untie her. She massaged her legs, bringing the circulation back.

He got out of bed to move the mirror. But before he did, she took one last look, this time at her post-sex appearance. She was a tousled mess, but she was flushed with satisfaction, too, pink and dewy, like a pollinated flower.

"Ready for sleep?" he asked.

She nodded, and they settled between the torn sheets. He pressed the front of his body to the back of hers, resting his arms gently around her waist. Slipping into a state of bliss, she allowed herself the luxury of loving him.

The spooning lasted a good ten minutes or so, and for Noah that seemed monumental. Even after he rolled over and put a gap between them, Jenny didn't lose faith. This was the kind of bonding she'd been waiting for. To her, it unveiled the human side of his DNA and his ability to get close to a woman.

Eleven

Noah's cell phone rang across the room, rousing him from sleep. He turned toward Jenny. Apparently the sound had awakened her, too. Their groggy gazes met.

"Are you going to answer that?" she asked.

He shook his head. "I don't feel like talking to anyone." He was far more interested in his lover and how compelling she looked with the threadbare sheet wrapped around her naked body. But after last night, why wouldn't he be enthralled with her? The "Beauty and the Beast" game had been tons of twisted fun.

The annoying chime finally quit. Silence really was golden. Not only was the room quiet, sunshine streamed through the window sheers, casting an amber glow.

"We should come back to this place another time," he said.

Her voice sparkled, complementing the glittery light. "I'd love to." She paused with a concerned expression. "But do you think they'll let us after what you did to the bed?"

"That's nothing. Rock stars trash entire hotel rooms."

"Yes, but you rented the castle for a private masquerade. Aren't they going to think that you took your character a bit too far?"

"I already warned them that I was a method actor. And I gave them a black card, the American Express with the highest spending power. They won't have any trouble charging me for the damages."

"I'll bet a forensic expert would be intrigued by the claw marks." She ran her finger along one of the cuts. "They're consistent with that of a mountain lion, only they fit a human hand."

"Listen to you, the zoologist detective. Thing is, Ms. Big Cat Canyon, the police aren't going to be called in. This isn't a crime scene."

She smiled. "My corset and petticoat say otherwise."

He smiled, too, and just as he prepared to kiss her, his phone blasted again.

"Someone is anxious to talk to you," she said.

"It might not even be the same caller."

"You should at least see if it is."

He waited until it quit ringing so it could go to voice mail; then he got out of bed and strode over to the desk, where the phone was. He checked the notifications. "It was Coyote. Both times." Figured. Who else would be so persistent? "He left messages both times, too." He listened to them and cursed beneath his breath. "He said that he's been trying to reach you. That it's important."

"Really? I left my phone in my room. Can I call him back on yours?"

He frowned at her. "Did you tell him that we went away together?"

"No. Did you?"

"No." And he wasn't inclined to hand over the phone, either. "You hold tight, and I'll call him." He scrolled his contacts list and tapped the other man's name.

Coyote answered right away and Noah said, "What's going on?"

"I'd rather talk to Jenny. Do you know where she is?"

"She's with me."

"Then put her on."

"I can relay whatever it is."

"All right. But don't get testy."

"Just spill it."

"I came up with a plan about how to find out more about the woman in Mexico."

Noah tightened his jaw. "Which is?"

"I think Jenny should consult Sienna."

"Sienna isn't going to know anything. She can't get readings on me."

"True. But she should be able to get a reading on Jenny, and since you two are connected by your dream, I figured it was worth a shot."

Noah glanced at Jenny. She was perched on the edge of the bed, all eyes and all ears. She was still clutching the torn sheet, and her ragged beauty was a distraction he didn't need, not while Coyote was blabbing about a troublesome topic. He turned away from her.

Coyote continued, "I already told Sienna that Jenny knows the truth about you, and she's willing to help. She even said that it's okay if Jenny knows the truth about her."

"Why would she agree to something like that?"

"She was fascinated by the *sapiya* and thinks that if they trust Jenny, then she should, too. Sienna is going to try to contact the *sapiya* during the reading."

Coyote sounded so proud and smug, Noah wanted to cram the phone up his butt. "I really hate that you're enjoying this."

"I can't wait to see what the end result is." An annoying chuckle, then, "I've been trying to envision you being mortal, growing into a grumpy old man and whatnot. Oh, wait—you already are a grumpy old man. You just look young and spry."

"You're a laugh a minute."

"At least I have a sense of humor. You need to loosen up, Noah."

Loosen up? While his immortality was being bandied about?

"Tell Jenny that I'll arrange a meeting with Sienna for next week," Coyote said. He ended the conversation with a silly, "Tootles," and the line went dead.

Noah pushed the Power button and shut the damn thing off. He shifted his gaze back to his lover.

She immediately said, "I heard you mention Sienna. Isn't she the redhead from the club who dresses up like a vampire? Why were you and Coyote talking about her? And what does she have to do with me? And what did you mean by a reading?"

"She doesn't just dress like a vampire. She *is* a vampire. She's also psychic, and Coyote spilled the beans and told her about my dream and your connection to it. So now she's interested in doing a reading for you to see if she can uncover anything about the woman in Mexico."

"Oh, my goodness. A supernatural psychic?"

"She can only read humans and other vampires. But according to Coyote, she's fascinated by the *sapiya* and trusts you because of them. She hopes to use them as a catalyst for the information you're seeking."

"Wow. This is something."

Yeah, it was something, all right. "I'm attending the reading with you." Noah wasn't about to let this go down without being present. Not only because he wanted to know everything that would be said and done, but also because he didn't think it was a safe environment for Jenny without him.

Sienna lived in a downtown loft. It was an unnerving place, Jenny thought, as she and Noah entered the building. Blacked-out windows, dark-paneled walls, and maroon satin drapery made the tightly closed lobby seem like the inside of a giant coffin. She doubted that Sienna was the only vampire who resided here. The lofts were probably filled with bloodsuckers from Noah's club, maybe even some who weren't members of his establishment.

She tightened the jacket around her shoulders.

"Did you catch a chill?" he asked.

"I'm just glad you're here with me."

"I figured you would be." Before they approached a gated elevator, he added, "We can leave now before you get in any deeper than you already are."

"I want to keep going." Bailing now didn't make sense. It was too late to go back in time and undo her feelings for Noah, even if the outcome was uncertain, even if she didn't have the courage to tell him that she hadn't heeded his don't-love-me warnings. "I want to know why the *sapiya* involved me in your dream."

"Yeah, and here we are on the verge of letting a vampire use her psychic voodoo to try to contact them. Lest you forget that they have the power to turn on any one of us?"

"I haven't forgotten what they're capable of, but we're not doing this out of disrespect. And apparently Sienna isn't worried about what they'll do or she wouldn't have offered the reading."

"She isn't the one whose immortality is being threatened."

Jenny looked closely at him. He was in human form, and the

shadowy surroundings created a ghostly effect, accentuating the hollow ridges of his cheekbones.

"Are you afraid of being mortal again?" she asked.

He scowled. "What kind of question is that?"

"When my interest in saving you first came up, you scoffed at it, and now you're referring to it as a threat."

"I'm just tired of being the butt of Coyote's joke."

"So you don't think there's even the remotest possibility that I'm capable of saving you?"

A muscle in his jaw ticked. "No."

"I think you do."

"You're accusing me of lying?"

"I didn't mean it that way."

"If you keep pushing my buttons, I'm going to take off right now and let you fend for yourself tonight."

Instinctively, she touched the pulse at her neck. What would she do if an unknown vampire sniffed her out? Or if Sienna got the blood-hungry urge to take a little nip out of her?

"Are you done being a know-it-all?" he asked.

She nodded, and they entered the elevator. He pulled the gate closed. Up they went, to the second floor.

The hallway led to three doorways. The last one belonged to Sienna. Noah knocked, and the sound of his knuckles hitting the wood echoed in Jenny's ears.

Sienna answered, wearing an emerald-green crushed-velvet

dress, no shoes, glitter-painted toenails, and costume jewelry. Her thick red hair danced over her shoulders and down her back. Cranberry lipstick, black eyeliner, and a sprinkling of ladylike freckles stood stark against a porcelain complexion.

"Come in," she said.

After they accepted the invitation, she approached Noah with a hug. Jenny's hug followed, and as Sienna lingered over the embrace, their breasts touched.

"You can let go now," Noah said to the vampire.

"Oh, sorry. Human flesh. It's just so divine."

He replied, "Yes, I know. But her flesh belongs to me."

Being talked about in a possessive manner made Jenny feel like a pet on a leash. But it also gave her a jolt of arousal, and she imagined taking off her clothes and offering herself to Noah in front of Sienna.

Suddenly the redhead shot her a playful smile, and her pulse quickened. Could Sienna read her thoughts?

"Yes, darling, I can," the psychic said. "Especially when it involves things like that."

Oh, God.

"What the fuck's going on?" Noah asked.

"Just girl talk," Sienna told him. "Right, Jenny?"

She jerked out a nod.

Sienna reached for her hand. "Come, let's sit at my table and see what kind of mischief we can conjure."

They were already conjuring mischief. As soon as Jenny's

gaze strayed to the bedroom, which was an open area in the corner, she pictured herself kneeling on the bed, with Noah mounting her doggie-style.

The vampire squeezed her hand, and Jenny's nerves tumbled. Why couldn't she keep her dirty thoughts to herself?

Noah followed the females, and the silent trio gathered at a wrought-iron table with a tiled-mosaic top.

Struggling to cool her sexual heels, Jenny focused on the mystical décor. Tapestries colored the walls and Persian rugs decorated the floor. Like the lobby, the windows had been blackened.

Sienna started the reading. "Think about the *sapiya*," she said to Jenny. "Visualize them in your mind."

"I've never seen them. I only know what Noah has told me."

"Then think about that."

Jenny concentrated. Little magic stones that can jump around like fleas and multiply by themselves. Stones you have to catch and feed and water. Stones that attract other people and bring anyone you want to your door.

"That's good," the psychic said. She lit a pink candle that was on the center of the table, and a cherry-blossom scent filled the air.

"This is stupid," Noah grumbled.

He received a glare from Sienna. "What's the matter with you? Are you afraid that I'll uncover something you won't want to hear?"

Ha. Jenny shot him a look, too. "I think he's afraid of being mortal again."

He shifted into cat mode and snarled at her. She flinched,

wishing she'd kept her mouth shut, particularly when Sienna reprimanded Noah with a snakelike hiss. The redhead's fangs popped out and her delicate features turned gargoyle-ish.

Jenny reached for the edge of the table and gripped it. Vampires weren't the least bit pretty when they were mad. Noah was none too pretty, either. He flashed his claws and growled at Sienna. Jenny's grip tightened.

The power struggle raged on, until Sienna pulled a fast one and threw Noah off-kilter. She arrogantly crooned, "Your lover wants to fuck you in front of me."

Jenny paled as he whipped his head toward her. She could actually feel the color leaving her face. Talk about being thrown under the bus.

"Is that true?" he asked.

"It was just a fantasy. I wasn't going to act on it."

His fire-gold gaze bored into hers. "Maybe *I* should act on it. Maybe I should yank you onto my lap and have at it right now."

Sienna interjected, "Her fantasy was doggie-style in my bed. And I'd be more than glad to participate, to lie beneath her and fondle her clit."

"I'm not sharing her with you," he snapped.

The vampire hissed, and the cat/man growled again. With equal intensity, they jumped out of their chairs, preparing to battle over Jenny as if she were a morsel of fresh meat.

"Stop!" A cluster of voices came out of the air simultaneously. But that wasn't the only jarring occurrence. An invisible force slammed Noah and Sienna back in their seats, treating them like bickering children on a time-out.

Their stunned expressions would have been comical if Jenny hadn't been just as startled.

Sienna recovered first. "It's the *sapiya*," she announced, returning to her pretty self.

Noah shifted into a calm exterior, too, and the little stones manifested into physical form. Jenny stared at them. They looked like typical pebbles you would find on the ground, only they were jumping around on the table. Some were even hopping over the candle, playing tag with the flame.

Sienna reached out to touch one, but it moved so fast, she couldn't get anywhere near it, proving how difficult they were to catch.

"We don't belong to you," their collective voices said to her.

"Who do you belong to?" she asked.

"No one."

Like a medium with a prized ghost, the psychic conducted the interview. "Tell me about the woman in Mexico who turned Noah into what he is."

"Her name is Lareina. It means 'the queen' in Spanish."

Sienna quickly proceeded. "*Is* she a queen of some sort?"

While the question hovered, Jenny scooted to the edge of her seat, anxious to know everything about Lareina. She glanced at Noah. He was fixed on the conversation, too.

But the *sapiya* didn't respond.

Sienna frowned, but forged ahead. "How did Lareina become a shapeshifter?"

Jenny waited, praying the little stones would cooperate. But they didn't. Once again, they chose not to answer.

Sienna prompted them. "Why aren't you giving us the information we're looking for?"

"We told you her name."

"Yes, but we want to know more."

"Then find Lareina and ask her."

"How?"

Yes, how? Jenny thought, as her heart pounded in anticipation. The question was ignored.

Sienna worked a different angle. "Why did you come to Noah in a dream and why did you tell him to reveal the truth about himself to Jenny?"

Another looming question. Everyone waited.

The *sapiya* danced in little circles. Then they said, "Because she has blood ties to the magic."

Jenny heard Noah's sharp intake of air. She sucked in a breath, too.

"What magic?" Sienna asked.

The twirling stones didn't reply. They jumped up, one by one, and vanished as abruptly as they'd appeared, extinguishing the cherry-blossom candle in their wake.

In the wax-dripping silence, Sienna looked at Jenny. Noah did, too.

"Read her," he said to the psychic. "Tap into the blood tie."

"I'm trying, but I can't feel her energy anymore. The *sapiya* must have blocked it from me."

"Fuck." He stood up and pushed away from the table. "So now what? We're supposed to theorize?"

"Or figure out how to find Lareina," Jenny said.

Noah got angrier. "I don't give a flying crap about Lareina or the magic you're tied to. All I wanted was a goddamn affair with you."

Sienna came to Jenny's defense. "Don't take this out on her. I think we should all just play nice and let off some steam in bed."

He rounded on the redhead. "We're not having a fucking threesome. I already told you that my prey isn't up for grabs."

"Your prey?" she taunted him. "Are you sure she doesn't mean more to you than that? For a man who only wanted an affair, you're awfully territorial about her."

"Because I don't want you feeding on her clit? For all I know, you'll turn her into a vampire behind my back."

Sienna rolled her eyes. "Go," she said to Jenny. "Take him out of here, and use your magic blood tie against him if you can. It would serve him right."

Jenny didn't want to use anything against anyone. Her feelings for Noah hadn't changed. She loved him, and based on his asinine behavior and Sienna's observant remark, she suspected that he was falling in love with her, too.

Twelve

Noah got behind the wheel and slammed his door shut. Jenny was already buckled into the passenger seat. He should've shared her with Sienna. He should've proved that he didn't give a damn if the vampire played with his prey.

The woman with blood ties to the magic.

Annoyed and confused, he started the engine. The Jaguar roared to life. It was the vehicle he'd offered to let Jenny drive. He remembered mentioning it to her when she'd first given him a tour of the rescue. That was when he'd been in control, or when he'd *thought* he'd been in control. If he knew then what he knew now, he wouldn't have embarked on this affair.

Yeah, well, so much for hindsight. He peeled away from the curb and into traffic.

"Where are we going?" she asked.

"I'm taking you home."

"Are you going to stay the night with me?"

Was she serious? "No."

"This isn't my fault."

"Yes, it is. You and your notions about saving me." But what did he expect? She rescued wildcats for a living. So why wouldn't she become hell-bent on rescuing a shapeshifter, too?

She set her chin. "I don't care if you're mad. I'm still going to pursue this. I'm going to find Lareina."

He entered the freeway on-ramp. "How? By Googling her? Maybe she has a Facebook profile. That would be handy, wouldn't it? You could send her a friend request."

She ignored his sarcasm. "My blood tie could be to her. She could be the magic the *sapiya* were referring to."

His annoyance worsened. "You'd like that, wouldn't you? Being connected to the bitch who tore me up."

"What an awful thing to say."

She was right. It was. Instead of apologizing, he punched the gas pedal, whipping through the night.

She shot him a warning. "You're going to get a ticket if you keep that up."

That triggered an urge to go faster, but the last thing he needed on this aggravating evening was a confrontation with the law.

He reduced his speed and reined in his anger. "I'm sorry, okay?

I shouldn't have said what I did. But what if you really are supposed to break a curse and make me mortal? How would I adapt?"

She gentled her tone. "You could move in with me and help me run Big Cat Canyon."

Cripes. The happily-ever-after thing. "And how long would that last? How long before we got tired of each other?"

"I'd never get tired of you."

"You'd think differently when I'm old and gray."

"No, I wouldn't. I'd be old and gray, too." Her voice remained soft. "The truth of the matter is, I love you, Noah. I tried to fight it. But I can't help how I feel."

If his hands hadn't been firmly planted on the wheel, he would've run into the side rail. "I'm already freaked-out, Jenny. I didn't need to hear that."

"Then should I wait to tell you the second part of it?"

"Is it worse than the first part?"

"It will be to you."

"Then yeah, you should wait." His gut was already coiling into a knot, and the taillights in front of him threatened to blur beneath his stony gaze.

She stayed quiet and let him drive.

Once they arrived at her house, he killed the engine, and they sat in the car. He unbuckled his seat belt, freeing himself from its tight hold. She undid hers, as well.

"Go ahead. Tell me the rest of it."

"You're going to say that I'm wrong. But I think that you're falling in love with me, too. Sienna probably thinks so, too."

He didn't like this, not for one heart-slamming minute. He narrowed his eyes at her. "So now you're an authority on what a psychic vampire is thinking?"

"She isn't the issue, Noah."

"No. I am." And he wasn't the fall-in-love type. Was he? At this stage, he didn't know what the hell was happening. But whatever it was, he should hightail his ass back home and try to decompress.

But then she said, "Come inside," beckoning him to stay. And damn if he wasn't swayed.

They exited the car, and although her porch was only a few feet away, he could've been walking along the edge of an enormous cliff. One misstep and he was screwed.

"Maybe I should just kiss you good night at the door."

"No, you should come in. And when did you get so proper?" She grabbed his hand, tugging him forward. "You sound like you're from another century."

He didn't appreciate her wisecrack, cute as it was. "Would you prefer a good-bye fuck at the door? I could do that just as easily."

"Don't be that way." She unlocked the door in question and flipped on a light switch, bringing her simple ranch furnishings into view.

Noah refused to imagine himself living here and running the rescue with her. She turned to face him, and he contemplated the blood tie.

He said, "You don't look anything like Lareina, but I suppose she could be an ancestor of yours."

"Maybe I should Google her. Maybe that wasn't such a bad idea, after all."

"How is that going to help? All you have is her name."

"It's a start. If she is or was a queen of some sort, maybe something will turn up."

She sat at the computer, and he stood behind her. The last time they were here together, he'd been Googling castles, and now she was searching for the possibility of royal bloodlines.

How ironic was that?

She looked and looked, but nothing surfaced. In spite of what the name meant, she couldn't find a queen called Lareina. Not a real one. Not a mythical one. *Nada.*

Leaving the computer behind, they moved over to the sofa. "There has to be a way to locate her," Jenny said. "Or else why would the *sapiya* have said to talk to her?"

"Who knows? But have you considered what type of dialogue that would be? Or how it would take place? Somehow I don't see her chatting with you over afternoon tea. You should just leave this alone. Let it go."

"I can't. You even said it yourself earlier: What if I'm meant to break a curse and make you mortal?"

He dropped his head back against the sofa. He didn't know what to think. Or what to feel. Other than flustered.

She said, "Maybe I should start working on a family tree. It might be a way to uncover if I have any blood ties to Lareina. Or if any of my other ancestors were involved in magic."

"That sounds like a major undertaking. It could take months. Or years. This could go on and on." He sat forward, tensing his muscles. "I'll give you a week."

"For the family tree?"

"For everything."

"You mean to find Lareina and break the curse, if there is one? You can't put that type of pressure on me."

"What about the pressure you're putting on me? Telling me that you love me, putting ideas in my head that I feel the same way about you. Get it done, Jenny. Either make me mortal by next week or stop this quest of yours."

Her gaze locked with his. "I'm not following an ultimatum like that."

"Then maybe I should end our affair right now."

"You'd do that?"

Confused about what to do, he went silent.

"Answer me, Noah. Please."

Her pleading tone made him think of how she'd begged him in bed, of how hot and beautiful and thrilling she was. He breathed in her sweet scent, pulling it through his nostrils and into his lungs.

Cursing the need to be near her, he said, "I'm not going to end it." Before he painted himself into corner, he added, "But I will when I'm good and ready."

"What if I *could* make you mortal by next week? Would you quit acting like a jerk and accept our life together?"

One minute she was worried about losing him and the next she was calling him a jerk? "You just blew it, Jenny. The week deal is off. I'm not accepting it under any circumstances."

She got up and went back to the computer. "I don't care what you say. I'm making you mortal with or without your permission."

"By spending all of your free time on genealogy sites? Who cares who your tenth cousin, fifteen times removed, is? Unless it's someone magical, of course. Really, truly, good luck with that. I'm sure you're going to need it."

"You're just mad because you don't want to admit that you have feelings for me. And stop hovering. I need to focus."

"Does it look like I'm hovering?" He headed for the kitchen to see what she had in the fridge.

Pasting a sandwich together, he slapped roast beef and cheese between two slices of rye bread. He grabbed an apple and poured a glass of ice water, too. Falling in love wasn't an option and he wasn't going to let her convince him otherwise.

Upon his return, he set the snack on the coffee table and reached for the remote.

She spun around in her chair. "Don't you dare turn on the TV. The noise will distract me."

"Jesus, woman. Could you sound any more like a nagging wife?"

"Is that your he-man way of proposing to me? Sorry, but you're going to have to do better than that."

As if. "Get over yourself, Beauty."

"Be prepared to grow old, Beast."

Verbal fencing. He took the final jab. "You wish." He glanced in the direction of the hallway. "I'm going to help myself to the TV in your room."

"Go ahead."

Food in tow, he kicked back on her bed and watched a reality show. But it wasn't nearly as colorful as his and Jenny's lives. If they had cameras following them around, the world would be shocked. Hell, he was shocked. This was a particularly strange night.

And it was about to get stranger.

Jenny came rushing in. "I heard a noise at the window. I think someone is out there."

He jumped up and followed her to the living room. They stood and listened. Indeed, something or someone was tapping on the glass.

He reacted like the man of the house, even if he had no intention of being the man of the house. "I'll go see what's going on."

"I'm coming with you."

Apparently she was afraid to stay inside alone. Noah opened the front door, descended the porch steps, and walked around the side of the building, with Jenny creeping behind him.

He stopped in his tracks when he saw who the tappers were. Jenny peered out from around his shoulder.

She gave a little gasp. "It's the *sapiya*."

It most certainly was. They were launching themselves at the window, much in the way a boy would toss pebbles to get a girl's attention.

"Do you think they know we're standing here?"

"Of course they do. They just haven't acknowledged us yet."

"What should we do?"

"Stay here until they decide to talk to us."

"I wish they would hurry up. This is making me nervous."

Him, too, but he wasn't about to admit it out loud.

In the midst of their game, the little stones multiplied. When they hit the glass, one would become two; then two would become three and so forth.

Soon there were hundreds of them.

Swarming like bees and glowing like fireflies, they flew straight at Noah and Jenny. He expected to get pelted. Apparently she did, too. She latched onto him for support.

But the *sapiya* didn't stone them. They stopped just short of an attack and formed a giant heart in the air.

A freaking heart, Noah thought. Wasn't Jenny accusing him of loving her enough? Did the *sapiya* have to remind him of it, too? Naturally, she seemed mesmerized by the romantic symbol. He would've preferred being pelted.

"Jenny?" the *sapiya* said.

"Yes?" she responded.

"We can bring Lareina to you. All you have to do is catch one of us."

Boom. Zoom.

The heart exploded into separate pieces, and the *sapiya* sped off. Jenny ran after them.

Noah was fast on her heels, but not for long.

Thud.

There it was: the same invisible force that had shoved him into his chair at Sienna's house. Only now it surrounded him like a giant bubble, containing him within it.

Fuck.

The *sapiya* didn't want him interfering with Jenny's attempt to make a catch.

Infuriated, he shifted into lion mode, snarling and snapping, even though he knew it wouldn't help. He would remain powerless until the force let him go.

He couldn't see Jenny anymore. "What if she falls and gets hurt?" he said to the disembodied energy that held him. Her property was laden with low-hanging trees, stiff shrubbery, and dirt paths. A danger zone in the dark.

His concern was ignored.

He didn't know how much time had passed. Ten minutes? Twenty? Finally he was released, and he dashed into the brush and picked up on Jenny's scent.

He found her on the ground. She *had* stumbled, and she *was* hurt. One of her pant legs was torn and her knee was bleeding. He swept her into his arms. "I would've come sooner, but the *sapiya* wouldn't let me."

"I couldn't catch any of them. I chased them until I fell. Then they were gone."

"If they show up again, you need to tell them that you changed your mind and you don't want to pursue Lareina."

"But I haven't changed my mind."

He carried her into the house. "Don't you see how dangerous this is? It's not worth it." He set her on the edge of the bathroom counter, shifted back to human form, and opened her medicine cabinet, looking for antiseptic and bandages. He noticed them on the bottom shelf. "If the *sapiya* brings Lareina here, she could kill you."

"Why would she, especially if I have blood ties to her?"

"And what if you don't?" He removed her shoes and helped her out of her jeans so he could treat her wound. "What if she's not the magic you're connected to?"

"I know it's risky. But I'll figure out a way to keep Lareina from hurting me."

"How?"

"I don't know."

"Oh, gee, that's reassuring." He smoothed her hair and discovered a leaf that had gotten lodged there. "I don't want anything bad to happen to you, Jenny."

"I'll be careful."

He discarded the leaf, picking away the crinkled pieces. "The way you were careful when you ran off in the dark and cut yourself?"

She leaned forward and kissed him. "Thank you for caring."

He held her close. "This doesn't mean that I love you."

"I think you do, and I think the *sapiya* were trying to tell you the same thing."

That damned heart. "And what good did that do? You still ended up on your ass."

"Next time I won't."

"You're getting cocky."

"Maybe I'm just feeling strong because of the magic in my blood."

She didn't look particularly strong, not in a T-shirt and cotton panties and a Band-Aid on her knee.

He helped her off the counter and led her to bed, insisting that she get some sleep.

Later, as they lay beside each other in the pitch of dark, he hoped her so-called strength didn't backfire on both of them.

Jenny sat across from Noah at her scarred kitchen table. She'd stayed awake for most of the night, wracking her brain about the Lareina dilemma and finally coming up with a solution.

She said, "After breakfast, will you go to the rescue with me?"

"What for?"

"To talk."

"About what?" He frowned. "And why can't we talk here?"

"I have an idea on how to keep Lareina from hurting me and it involves the rescue. So I'd rather discuss it on-site."

He agreed to accompany her, and she took him to an area with an empty enclosure.

She said, "We use this as temporary housing to separate an animal for social or health reasons. That's why it's smaller than our primary enclosures. I want to use it for Lareina. I think it'll be a safe place to keep her."

He more or less gaped at her. "And just how do you intend to get her into a cage?"

"I'm going to ask the *sapiya* to put her there, and after I'm done talking to her, they can send her back to wherever she came from."

He obviously wasn't impressed. "*That's* your idea?"

"What's wrong with it?" To her, it sounded as plausible in practice as it was in theory.

He shot it full of holes. "You'd have to catch one of the *sapiya* first, and even if you're able to accomplish that and they're able to put Lareina in a cage, you can't control how she behaves or if she'll talk to you. And what if someone on your staff sees her when she's in human form and reports you for having a woman locked up?"

Jenny patched the holes. "She won't be in the enclosure long enough for anyone to see her. I'll have the *sapiya* bring her here after hours. As for her refusing to talk to me, I'll tell her that if she doesn't cooperate, I'll turn their magic against her."

"You're putting a lot of stock into those stones and just how far they'll be willing to go for you."

"If I catch one of them, I'll be its owner. Then it will have to listen to me, won't it?"

"As long as it thinks your requests are reasonable. And there's no guarantee that the *sapiya* will reappear and even give you a chance at ownership."

"Stop discouraging me. At least I came up with a plan."

Noah approached the enclosure. "If you are able to get Lareina here, I wonder if being locked up is going to set her off, if she'll pace and snarl the whole time. If it was me, I'd go stir crazy. I'd lose my mind."

She moved closer, standing beside him. She recalled his aversion to cages. "It's not going to be you."

The sun beat down from the sky, glinting off his jet-black hair. "Lareina's motives never mattered to me before, but now I can't help but wonder: Did she choose me randomly or was I part of a bigger picture from the start?"

"I don't know, but those are some of the questions I intend to ask her."

"It was easier not caring. It was easier before I met you, Jenny."

Because she was changing him, she thought, bringing his emotions to the surface. "It was easier for me before I met you, too." She talked a good talk about making him mortal, but what if she couldn't do it?

After a stretch of silence, she said, "Don't you think it's strange that we haven't heard from Coyote yet? Seems to me he would be chomping at the bit to find out what happened at Sienna's house."

"He probably already talked to her about it."

"I'm going to call him later and fill him in on the rest of it."

"I'd prefer that you leave him out of it."

"If he hadn't arranged the meeting with Sienna, I wouldn't know about the blood tie and the *sapiya* probably wouldn't have offered to help. Coyote is part of this, whether you like it or not."

"What about the family tree? Are you still going to mess with that?"

She nodded. "I'm not going to leave any stone unturned. No pun intended."

He changed the subject. "Let's go to the club tonight. Let's clear our thoughts and have some fun."

Curious, she asked, "Do you have something special in mind?"

"Actually, I do. We can watch other people play in the sensation center, and afterward, we can play privately in my apartment. You and me and the sex toy of my choice."

Her blood went thick and warm. "Which is?"

"I'll tell you when the time comes." Territorial as ever, he pulled her into his arms.

Making her glad that she belonged to him.

The sensation center fascinated Jenny. The massive room offered sparkly walls and an array of beds, which were out in the open, and, according to Noah, had to be reserved ahead of time.

Lovers pleasured themselves or their partners in a multitude of ways. Vibrators, masturbators, massage oils, silky fabrics, feathers, metal spurs. The list went on and on. But the most curious, at least to Jenny, was the use of a sex doll.

A trio of women in mermaid costumes spritzed water at one another, via spray bottles, as their groupie, a male doll dressed in a vintage sailor suit, shared their bed. With his tousled hair, tanned skin, slight beard stubble, and intricate eyelashes, he looked amazingly lifelike. He also had a thundering erection popping out of his pants.

"The doll of dolls," Jenny said.

Noah responded, "It's made from silicone and has a skeletal frame with flexible joints. I think it cost around six grand. They pooled together to buy it."

"That's certainly a far cry from the blow-up kind."

"Those are still around, mostly as gag gifts. But there are some in-between models, too, made of latex. Just about anything you're looking for is available now."

"Gosh, who knew?"

"The first sex dolls originated in the seventeenth century and were fashioned from cloth. French and Spanish sailors used them on long sea voyages. The dolls were female, of course."

She glanced at the mermaids. "So they dress their boy toy like a sailor? That's a clever role reversal." She took a closer look at the women and recognized one of them. "I remember her from my first night at the club. I saw her in the lobby. She's really beautiful."

"So are you." He kissed her, warm and slow, and she savored the feeling.

They separated, and she noticed that the mermaids were taking turns with their silicone groupie, kissing him the way Noah had just kissed her.

Intrigued, Jenny watched. It was oddly flattering to be mimicked in such a romantic way. Oddly arousing, too.

"Do they have actual sex with him?" she asked Noah.

"All the time. His dick is like a dildo, but with the rest of the body attached. Have you ever used a dildo?"

She shook her head, felt a zip of excitement. "Is that your sex toy of choice for tonight?"

He nodded. "I've got a big, brand-new one that's calling your name, and I want to fuck you with it."

The zip of excitement intensified. But she got nervous, too. "Just how big is it?"

"Big enough to look impressive, but not big enough to hurt you. It has clit-stimulating bumps, and it'll squirt any type of liquid."

Oh, my goodness. An ejaculating dildo. "What type of liquid are you going to use?"

"A recipe for fake cum." He nuzzled her ear. "And you can tell me exactly when I should squirt it. The moment it happens is up to you."

Jenny tingled, anxious to be the recipient of his liquid-spilling toy. "Can we go to your apartment now?"

"Absolutely."

After they entered his place, he produced the dildo. It was still

SHERI WHITEFEATHER

in its box. He opened the container and handed her the phallus, allowing her to examine it.

The soft, smooth head led to a ribbed neck and long, thick shaft, making it an anatomic wonder. The sensory bumps he'd mentioned were near the base, as was a squeezable bulb for the liquid.

She returned it to him, and he washed it at the kitchen sink. Then he got started on the fluid, warming it on the stove. Mostly it consisted of plain yogurt.

Jenny came up behind him and slipped her arms around his waist.

"What are you doing?" he asked.

"What does it feel like I'm doing?" She reached down and fondled him through his pants. She wanted to touch him while he was making cum.

His fly bulged beneath her hand. But soon he pulled away, reminding her that his cock wasn't the toy they'd be playing with tonight. After the fluid was ready, he filled the dildo.

They went to his room and he told her to strip. She peeled off her garments, tossed them aside, and waited for another instruction.

"Get in bed," he said. "On your hands and knees."

"You're going to do this to me doggie-style?"

"After your fantasy at Sienna's house, hell yes, I am."

She assumed the position, her heart gathering speed. "Are you ever going to let me live that down?"

"No." He got behind her.

His nearness stirred a rush of exhilaration, and her pussy clenched in anticipation. He ran the dildo along her spine. He kept rubbing, caressing, heading toward his target.

Then he stopped.

"Noah."

"Hold on. I'm getting the lube."

She stared at the wall in front of her.

Waiting . . .

Oh, sweet damn. The solution was warm and slick and so were his fingers. Instinctively, she widened her knee stance, preparing for the dildo.

One, two, three . . .

Inch by inch, he made penetration.

He moved it in and out, then shifted the angle. Jenny sucked in a breath. The bumps hit their mark, massaging her clit. Whoever designed that feature knew what he or she was doing. Noah knew exactly how to manipulate it, too.

She moaned in fuck-me pleasure. "Now I'm really in love with you."

He pushed the device deeper. "Don't talk about love."

"I can't help it."

"It screws with my head."

And he was screwing with her heart. She envisioned him in her mind's eye, thrusting the toy. "Do you have to make it come all at once or can you give me a sample?"

"You mean like this?" He shot a stream of the homemade fluid into her.

"Yes. Just like that." The milky wetness assailed her senses. The fucking motion. The stimulating bumps. It was all so heavenly. "Can we do this again sometime?"

"We're not done this time."

"I know. But it just feels so . . ." Caught in a crescendo of flutters, she rocked forward, verging on orgasm. She panted, "Make it squirt a little more."

He gave her what she wanted.

She asked for more.

Again, he gave it to her.

She told him to shoot the rest of it.

And he did. Oh, how he did. At the exact moment she was coming, he made the dildo fully come, too. Perfect timing. A strange and wild union. Jenny bucked and shuddered and collapsed on the bed.

Crazy in love.

Thirteen

Later that night, Jenny and Noah went skinny-dipping in his rooftop pool. With the moon shining in the sky and patio-style lights glimmering on the water, she relished the moment. But she relished every moment with him.

"You look like a mermaid," he said.

"Like the ladies at the club?" She slicked back her wet hair. "They're not real mermaids, are they?" She hadn't even considered the possibility until now.

He slicked back his hair, too. "How could they be real mermaids when they have legs?"

"Maybe they transform when they're in the ocean."

"They don't. They're just regular girls pretending to be mythical creatures."

She sat beside him on the steps of the pool. "So do mermaids exist?"

"Yes, but I've never met one."

"Then how do you know they exist?"

"Because I know everything about the supernatural world." He smiled, obviously teasing her. "I'm the king of my kind."

"You are not." She bumped his shoulder, teasing him right back. "If you were, you'd know who Lareina is and why she turned you into a shapeshifter."

His expression darkened. "I don't want to talk about Lareina, Jenny. Not tonight."

"I'm sorry. You're right. Tonight isn't supposed to be about her." She returned to the original topic. "Tell me more about mermaids."

"There are different breeds, so not all mermaids behave in the same manner. That's why the legends about them vary."

"Do all mermaids sing?"

"No."

"What else varies about them?"

"Some are kind to men and others will drown a man while pretending to rescue him. There is also a type of mermaid whose kiss can heal a sick human and whose tears have magical properties."

"I wonder what sorts of things would make a mermaid cry."

"I don't know."

Jenny sighed. "If I were a mermaid, I'd cry if I fell in love with a man. I'd want to become human so I could be with him."

"You and your romantic ideas."

"I wasn't like this until I met you, Noah."

"Or until Coyote put a fairy tale in your head. Most of this is his fault."

"I didn't fall in love with you because of Coyote or his rendition of 'Beauty and the Beast.' It helped trigger my quest to make you mortal, but what I feel for you developed on its own." She tapped her chest, where her heart beat against her breastbone. "It happened from spending time with you."

Noah went silent, and she studied his profile. Water dripped from his hair and onto his shoulders, creating diamond-like drops against his naturally bronzed skin.

He looked young and beautiful and immortal. Or maybe he looked immortal only because she knew that was what he was.

"Do mermen exist, too?" she asked.

He nodded. "The stories about them are similar to their female counterparts."

"What happens if a mermaid or merman is taken out of the water?"

"It depends on what type they are. In some cases, their tails will turn to legs. But they can't survive that way for very long. All mermaids and mermen need to be nourished by the sea, a lake, or a river, or they'll die."

She studied him again. "Are mermen handsome?"

"Why? Do you want to trade me in for one?"

"Why would I want to do that?"

"Because there is a type of merman who will become human if he marries a mortal woman."

"Oh, that's nice." She splashed a bit of water at him. "If only it was that easy with you."

He splashed her, too. "Keep it up and I'll turn you over to an ugly old merman."

"They can grow old?"

"Some breeds do."

"I wish I could see you grow old."

"Gee, thanks."

"I didn't mean that in a bad way."

He frowned. "I know how you meant it."

Suddenly she got an idea, a brainstorm. "We should try an age progression."

"What?"

"You know, one of those computer sites that ages photographs of people. Then I could see what you would look like if you became mortal. I could see you getting older. We could do it at my house, tomorrow night."

"Why would I agree to that?"

"To humor me."

"More like to feed your fantasy to make me mortal. No way, Jenny. I'm not interested."

She jabbed at his ego. "Maybe you're just afraid to see an older version of yourself."

He went macho. "I'm not afraid of anything."

"You're afraid of how I make you feel."

"I am not."

"Then come to my house tomorrow night and we'll do the age progression. *Please*."

"Oh, great. Now you're going to beg? You know it excites me when you beg."

She put her head on his shoulder. "Pretty please."

"You're going to have to do better than that."

She nipped his earlobe. "Pretty please with pineapple on top."

"You're bribing me with my favorite treat?"

"Whatever works." On the night she'd first gone to the club, he'd talked about rubbing chunks of pineapple on her and licking off the juice.

"Actually a full-on fruit salad would be good, with whipped cream and marshmallows. The whole bit."

She nipped him again. "Okay, then, pretty please with the whole bit on top."

"All right. I'll do the age progression with you tomorrow if you make a fruit salad with me tonight."

"Are we going to do sexy stuff with it?"

"Whatever works," he said, borrowing her line. He stood up and pulled her to her feet. "Let's make it now."

"Do you have everything we need?"

"Yep."

"Even the whipped cream and marshmallows?"

"Yes, ma'am, I do."

They dried off, put on their robes, and went back to his apartment. Once they were in the kitchen, they gathered the ingredients. Earlier he'd made a recipe for cum, and now they were fixing an erotic dessert.

He had lots of canned pineapple, along with canned pears and mandarin oranges. For fresh fruit, they used apples and bananas.

She cubed the apples and diced the bananas while he opened the cans and drained the juices. He also grabbed a jar of maraschino cherries.

"We can add some of these for a little pop-your-cherry zip," he said.

"My cherry has already been popped."

"Not your food-play cherry. This is the first time you've done anything like this, isn't it?"

She smiled. "Good point."

They combined the fruit in a big plastic bowl. He added the whipped cream, stirring it slowly. The marshmallows came next.

"Where are we going to eat this?" she asked, imagining the wonderful mess it was going to make.

He grabbed the bowl, but he didn't get any spoons. "In the shower."

They proceeded to the master bath, a room with a custom-built glass-block shower stall, framed in glossy black tiles.

"Get in," he told her.

She removed her robe and entered the stall. It was plenty big for two. Actually, it was big enough for three people.

"Have you ever had a ménage in here?" she asked.

He got naked and climbed inside, too. "I've never even had a twosome in here. No one uses this except me."

Her heart did a happy little flip. "I'm the first woman you've invited into your shower?"

"Yes, but don't make a deal of it. Now stand still, so I can cover you in dessert."

Oh, goodness. She took a deep, excited breath. She didn't care what he said. Being the first woman in his shower *was* a major deal. Apparently all of his other lovers had bathed in the guest bath, as she'd been doing up until now.

He took the entire salad and rubbed it all over her—across her chest, around her breasts, along her stomach, on the top of her mound, and down her legs.

Pineapples, pears, bananas, oranges, apples, cherries . . .

Frothy cream . . .

Little marshmallows . . .

"Do you want to taste it?" he asked.

She nodded.

He fed her some from his fingers, and then they kissed like fiends. It was the most beautiful kiss she could have imagined, wild and sweet and hungry.

Their bare bodies stuck together with fruit clinging between them and falling onto the shower floor.

When they separated, he started the sensual process of licking the treat from her skin.

He got on his knees to eat her, clutching her bottom while he did it, and marking her cheeks with whipped cream.

Was he leaving handprints on her ass?

She pitched forward, dizzy with the feeling. She ran her fingers through his pool-damp hair and got whipped cream in it. He sucked a marshmallow in his mouth and laved her labia.

Mercy. But she liked food play.

She glanced down and saw pineapples squished beneath her feet. She wiggled her toes.

Noah smiled. "Who knew you would be such a decadent girl?"

Yes, who knew?

She spread more whipped cream in his hair, and he did wicked things with his tongue. Then he shifted into lion mode and grazed her thighs with his canines.

She pitched forward again.

"Are you sure you want to make me mortal?" he asked. "I'm way more fun like this."

"Don't taunt me about that. Not now." She gripped his shoulders, digging her nails into his skin.

"Are you ready to come?" he asked.

"Yes."

"Then say it."

"I'm ready." She practically keened out the words.

He grazed her thigh again.

"Please," she said, desperate for him to put his tongue back inside.

"Sweet Jenny. Begging to be licked. I'm going to fuck you when this is over."

"Make me come first."

He did just that. He pleasured her, over and over, until she shook and shuddered and panted his name.

While she was recovering, he turned on the spigot and drenched her, and himself, in warm water.

Moments later, they kissed and scrubbed clean, with soggy bits of fruit floating around the drain. As promised, he fucked her. He pushed her against the shower wall and entered her with white-hot fury.

Taking her for the ride of her life.

Noah arrived at Jenny's house the following night, cursing himself for allowing her to mess with his life.

What was he doing with a woman who was hoping to make him mortal? A woman who claimed to love him, who insisted that he loved her, too?

"This is a mistake," he said.

"Come on, Noah. It's just an experiment, and I already joined the site. It's really easy. All you have to do is upload a picture and set the aging factors. It shows you the changes right away."

"Are you going to do a progression of yourself?"

"I already did, and I saved it on my computer. Do you want to see the results?"

Curious, he nodded. At the moment it was tough to envision Jenny growing old even if he knew it was going to happen to her.

She booted up her computer and opened the photo section. "This is the original. I took it of myself this morning."

He gazed at the image. It was a simple headshot, looking straight into the camera, with her hair pulled away from her face.

She said, "You're not supposed to smile. They need a picture with a neutral expression. Eyes open, mouth closed, and flat, even lighting."

Noah asked, "Where's the aged version of it?"

"Here." She opened another photo file. "It's a series of them." She clicked on the first one. "Me at thirty."

"You don't look any different."

"I know." She laughed a little. "But it's only two years from now." A second click. "This is me at forty."

The image was still beautiful, but definitely changed. Jenny, more mature. She would probably be a wife and mother at that stage of her life. He didn't want to think about who her husband would be. Casting himself in that role wasn't a fantasy he was willing to buy into, but envisioning her with someone else gave him a piercing feeling in his gut.

He didn't like this experiment.

She kept going. "This is me at fifty."

Would her kids be teenagers by then?

"Me at sixty."

The changes were much more significant now. Threads of gray in her hair, more pronounced lines on her face.

She said, "And finally, at seventy." She showed him the last image. "It's weird because my grandma never made it to seventy. Yet here's an idea of what I will look like. Technology is amazing, isn't it?"

Amazing. Disturbing. Noah had been born when photography was still a new medium, and now he was knee-deep in the computer era.

"It's time to do yours." She got her camera and aimed it at him. "Remember—don't smile."

"Do I look like I'm interested in smiling?"

"Actually, you look like an ogre."

As soon as she snapped the picture, he made a ridiculous face, ruining the shot.

"Hey!" She laughed.

He couldn't help but laugh, too. They obviously had the same silly sense of humor. "That's what you get for calling me an ogre."

"Be serious now."

He allowed her to take another picture, and this time he behaved, keeping a neutral expression.

She uploaded it onto her computer and logged in on the age-progression site. By now she was a pro. She obviously knew exactly how to use the software. Noah grabbed a chair and sat beside her.

After she put his picture into the system and it appeared on the screen, she created a profile on him that included his gender, current age, and ethnicity.

She narrated as she typed. "A twenty-eight-year-old Native American male."

The software didn't know that he'd been twenty-eight since the previous century, so it processed the information just fine.

"I wonder what would happen if we put in a picture of me as a shapeshifter?" he asked, as she proceeded with the setup.

"I guess it would age you looking like that. That would be strange, wouldn't it?"

It all was strange, as far as he was concerned.

She explained, "This program has effects you can add, like smoking, sun exposure, and obesity. I didn't use any of them on mine. I don't smoke, I wear sunscreen, and I don't plan on gaining a significant amount of weight."

"Most people don't."

"True." She smiled. "But I hope to stay active when I'm older."

"And I'm going to be an active twenty-eight-year-old forever," he quipped.

"Spoilsport."

"Hey, at least I'm letting you do this dang progression. And who wouldn't want to stay twenty-eight forever?"

"I wouldn't want to be a lonely twenty-eight-year-old for the rest of my life."

"I'm not lonely."

"That's because you have me. But when I'm too old to be your partner, you're going to be lonely for my companionship."

He frowned at the thought. He did enjoy being with her. He enjoyed it too damned much. "If we were meant to be a couple, we would have been born in the same era."

"Don't forget about my blood tie to the magic, Noah."

He didn't want to talk about the blood tie. "Come on, let's just do this."

"All right. Here we go." She didn't add any of the effects. She kept him as a nonsmoker, with minimal sun exposure, and no obesity.

Less than a minute later, the results were in. Noah at thirty, at forty, at fifty, at sixty, at seventy. He stared at each frame.

"This is freaky." He gestured to the fifty-year-old image, memories skimming the surface of his long-ago mind. "It looks like my dad. *Erke.*"

"Ith-Key?" She repeated it the way he pronounced it. "Was that your dad's name?"

"No. *Erke* means 'father' in my language. He was a good man. Strong. Proud. He hated living in Indian Territory. That's why he took us to Mexico with the Seminole rebellions. We were one of the last families to return to Indian Territory. He held out as long as he could."

She put her hand on his knee. "You must have looked like him when he was younger, too."

"Truthfully, I don't remember what he looked like when he was my age. But I was just a kid then."

"How many children were in your family? How many brothers and sisters did you have?"

"No brothers. I was the only son, the youngest. I had two older sisters. Emma and Lilly. They were both married with daughters of their own. My little nieces. My mother doted on them."

"You sound proud of them, too."

"They were sweet girls. Toddlers the last time I saw them." But their chubby young faces were just a blur. Everyone he'd once loved was misty to him. Like ghosts in the rain.

She kept her hand on his knee. "Your family must have wondered what happened to you. They must have been worried when you never returned from your trip."

"It doesn't matter now. The past is the past."

"I want a future with you, Noah."

"You want a future with him." He frowned at the age-enhanced images of himself. "But the man in those pictures doesn't exist."

"He does to me. And I'm going to find out why the *sapiya* connected us to each other."

"Are you still hell-bent on doing your family tree?"

She nodded. "You could do yours, too. You could find out who your descendants are."

He shook his head. He didn't want to know what happened to his nieces or their kids or grandkids. Nor did he want to know when his parents or his sisters had died. He'd buried them a long time ago in his mind.

"You can do whatever you want with your family," he said. "But I'm leaving mine alone."

Two days later, Jenny worked on her family tree. The Internet instructions she'd printed said to begin with a single surname or individual. Since her father had left before she'd been born and she knew virtually nothing about him or his family, she focused on her mother's side for now, using her grandpa as the "individual" whose roots she was tracing.

As evening rolled around, she sat on her living room floor with Matt, sorting through dusty old boxes. Her mom and Matt's dad had been siblings, so she'd asked her cousin to come to her house and bring old photos, documents, or anything else he might have on hand about their family. She gathered what she had, as well, a lot of which had come from the attic, where Grandpa had stored it.

"What's your sudden interest in creating a family tree?" Matt asked.

"It's just a bug I got." She wasn't about to tell him that she was searching for an ancestor who practiced magic because she was trying to make Noah mortal. Nor could she tell him about the *sapiya* or how they'd offered to help, if they ever showed up again.

Matt would think she'd gone bonkers.

He paged through a photo album, stopping to look at pictures of his parents. "This was about a year before they broke up. Talk about a bitter divorce. Then my dad goes and dies."

"I know. I'm sorry." His father suffered a heart attack soon after the divorce. Matt had just graduated from high school. "I know how hard it was on you."

"Grandpa had a tough time of it, too. First he loses Grandma, then your mom, then my dad."

Jenny nodded. By the time Grandpa passed away, his wife and both of his children were already gone.

Matt said, "Grandpa sure did right by us. Raising you the way he did and giving us what he could."

She nodded again. She'd received the house and the rescue, and Matt had been the beneficiary of a life insurance policy. "I still miss him."

"Me, too. I wonder what he would think of you doing a family tree?"

Or falling in love with a mountain lion shapeshifter? she thought. Taking a chance, she asked, "Did Grandpa ever mention anyone named Lareina to you?"

He scrunched up his face. "Not that I can recall. Why? Who is she?"

She fudged a response. "I'm not sure. But I seem to remember hearing the name."

"Wasn't one of our great-aunt's named Leanne or Luanne or something? Maybe you're mixing it up."

"Her name was Joanne. And she wasn't a blood relative. She was married into the family. I'm more interested in direct descendants."

"Is that what you think this Loraine lady is?"

"Lareina."

"That's what I meant." He got sidetracked by the photo album on his lap. He turned the page and grinned. "Hey, look at these. They're from my twelfth birthday. Check out the snowboard I got. Boy, is that a dinosaur now."

Jenny sighed. Trust Matt. Now he was prattling about every snowboard, skateboard, and surfboard he'd ever owned. He couldn't get Lareina's name right, but by damn, he knew what brand was what.

She studied her cousin. If she was connected to the magic, then he was, too, as long as it came from that side of the family. But somehow Matt didn't seem like part of it. Did that mean she was focusing on the wrong family?

For all Jenny knew, she was grasping at straws.

Hours later, after Matt left, she stretched her achy muscles, overwhelmed by it all. She wished the *sapiya* would reappear and provide the opportunity to chase them. Or better yet, she wished one of them would simply give itself to her.

Exhausted, she closed up the boxes. But before she shut the flap on the final box, a little stone jumped out and landed straight into her hand.

Making her wish come true instantly.

Fourteen

Jenny closed her hand around the stone, ensuring that it didn't pull a fast one and leap away.

"You're mine," she said. "I own you."

"Yes," a small lone voice answered.

Slowly she opened her hand and gazed at the *sapiya*. It sat motionless in her palm. "Thank you for giving yourself to me."

"You're welcome."

So polite. So sweet. Although its surface was plain, she imagined it with a happy face: dots for eyes and a curved line for a mouth.

"Put me in a container," it said. "Give me a home."

She considered what type of home it should have. Something

special, she decided. "I have a trinket box that belonged to my grandfather."

"That will be nice."

She carried the stone into her bedroom. "Is it all right if I set you down while I get it?"

"Yes."

She placed the *sapiya* on her dresser. The wooden box was on a shelf in her closet. She lifted it carefully and carried it over to the stone.

"Should I remove the contents before I put you in it?" She opened the hinged lid. "It's just some old coins and a few tie clips Grandpa wore when he was younger."

"The items can stay."

She placed the *sapiya* in its new home, which was lined in red velvet. It hopped around for a bit, then settled beside a tarnished-silver tie clip.

"I'll bring Lareina to you," it said.

She responded, "I have a plan regarding that."

After she explained, the *sapiya* said, "I'll put her in the empty enclosure at first light, before the rescue opens. Also, you should know that Lareina is not your ancestor. The magic descends from a woman named Taika."

"How am I related to Taika?"

"She comes from your father's side."

So she had been focusing on the wrong family tree.

The *sapiya* added, "Taika was a sorceress, and she cast a spell that turned Lareina into a shapeshifter."

"She cursed Lareina?"

"No. Lareina wanted to become a lion. She paid Taika for the spell. But it was an ancient incantation, not something that Taika formulated herself."

Jenny sat on the edge of the bed and placed the box next to her. "If my ancestor cast the spell, then that must mean I have the power to break it."

"Lareina can provide that information."

"What if she doesn't want me to break it? Are you sure I can trust her?"

"I will confirm if her responses are genuine."

Did that mean the *sapiya* knew as much about the spell as Lareina did? Nerves bundled with excitement. "Can I call Noah? Can he be there?"

"The conversation should be between you and Lareina. Noah's presence would complicate the matter."

"Then I'll do it on my own."

The stone moved to the other side of the box. "Before Taika died, she saw your face in a vision. She didn't know your name or what your future entailed, but she could tell that you were one of her descendants. Your resemblance to her was clear."

Jenny couldn't be more awed. "How do you know so much about Taika?"

"I used to belong to her."

She was equally awed about that. She hadn't expected such a deep connection. But it made sense why the *sapiya* had gotten involved in her life, too. "How did Taika die?"

"Of old age. I was at her bedside when she passed."

Touched by its loyalty, she smiled at the little stone, then gazed out the window. "I don't know what to do with myself before it turns light."

"Sleep, and I will wake you."

"I don't think I can."

"You will function better if you are well rested before Lareina arrives."

"Then I'll try." She got ready for bed, anxious for morning to come.

At dawn, Jenny drove to the rescue with the *sapiya* on the passenger seat. The little stone had awakened her, as promised, and now it was silent in its box.

She parked in her usual spot and walked the rest of the way toward the empty enclosures, carrying the *sapiya*. The lid was open on the box, and the tie clips and coins glittered beneath a pale mauve sky.

Shrubs grew alongside the dirt path, and when Jenny came to a profusion of tall plants, she stopped and plucked a large green leaf, recalling that the *sapiya* required fresh dew. She cupped the leaf and dripped the dew onto the stone. The water was immediately absorbed into its surface. Later she would give it blood, using meat from her refrigerator, as animal blood was the other sustenance it needed.

"Is Lareina already there?" she asked.

"No. She will appear after we arrive. You will see her manifest before your eyes."

Jenny continued walking. Soon the enclosure would come into view. "Will she appear as a woman or a lion?"

"A woman."

"I'm going to threaten to turn you against her if she doesn't cooperate with me."

"You can do whatever you feel is necessary."

She reached the empty enclosure and set the box on the ground. A bird flew overhead and the rush of wings made her flinch. Nonetheless she said to the *sapiya*, "I'm ready anytime you are." Even if her heart was pounding, even if her nerves were jumping.

She watched the enclosure and waited.

Lareina appeared. She had thick dark hair, seductive features, and a filmy dress clinging to her hourglass figure.

She gasped at her surroundings, spun around, and saw Jenny. She gasped again. Then she got downright indignant.

"What manner of devilry is this?" she asked in a Spanish-laced accent. "And why do you favor Taika?"

"I'm her descendant, and I want information about the spell she cast on you."

"What type of enchantress are you that you seek what you should already know?"

Jenny went for the threat. "I'm the type who can turn my magic against you."

Lareina took a cautionary step back. "What do you want to know about the spell?"

Rather than jump right into breaking it, Jenny replied, "First tell me about yourself and why you wanted to become a lion shifter."

"I was born in Mexico in the nineteenth century. I was a peasant girl with a regal name. When I was twenty, I was taken captive by a Mayan god. He mocked me, calling me queen of the slaves. I despised him."

Not much of a queen status, but it explained why her name was relevant. "Go on."

"I served him for five years, then he traded me to an Incan god, and I became his slave. He was no better than the Mayan. Then I caught the attention of a Sky Dweller who noticed me from afar. We forged a forbidden attraction. Our lust was strong. But we couldn't be together."

Jenny recalled what Noah had said about Sky Dwellers being lion shapeshifters who couldn't have sex with humans because their bodies were poisonous to each other.

"Soon the Incan god grew tired of me and sent me back to earth. The Sky Dweller couldn't forget me, and he began sneaking visits to my home. It was torturous because we desperately longed to mate. Anxious for a solution, I looked for a sorcerer who could turn me into what he was, or something similar, at least. That's what led me to Taika. She was an American living in Mexico City, and she had a powerful reputation."

"What happened to your relationship with the Sky Dweller?"

"He was banned from the sky because of our deception, but we are still together and very much in love."

It all sounded so nice, except this was the woman who'd ripped Noah to shreds. "You attacked a man outside of a cantina and turned him into what you are. His name is Noah, and *he* is the man I love."

Lareina cocked her head. "Taika told me that he never shifted completely."

"She checked on him?"

"Not in person. She looked into one of her crystals and saw him. Is he still half-cat?"

"Yes, and I want to know how I can break the spell to make him mortal again."

"You can't."

Jenny didn't believe her, but before she could look to the *sapiya* for the truth, Lareina added, "The spell Taika used had a stipulation: I had to turn one human male into a shifter. I had a month to accomplish the task or else I would revert back to being human. But none of the men I attacked survived, and I was running out of time. I kept searching for the right prey, combing all of Mexico. I chose Noah because I heard that his people possessed a special medicine."

The tiger medicine, Jenny thought.

Lareina continued, "When he survived, the spell was fully enacted. My immortality became infallible and so did his."

Jenny finally glanced down at the *sapiya*. "Please tell me she's lying."

The stone responded, "She speaks the truth."

Jenny's stomach sank, and Lareina walked over to the edge of the containment and peered down at the ground to see where the voice came from.

"Is that the magic you used to cage me?" she asked.

"Yes," Jenny said. For all the good it did.

"Make it release me."

"Not yet," the *sapiya* said.

Jenny didn't see why it mattered. What was the point of all this? The *sapiya*'s presence wasn't making sense anymore and neither was Lareina's. Jenny's dream of making Noah mortal had just shattered into a zillion useless pieces.

Lareina made a puzzled expression. "I don't understand."

Me neither, Jenny thought.

The other woman expounded. "Why are you fretting over an old spell? Why don't you create a new one and make yourself into a shapeshifter? Then you can be immortal, too."

Jenny's heart skipped. "Is that possible?" she asked the *sapiya*. Did she have sorcery powers that she wasn't aware of? "Can I do that?"

"No," it responded.

"Can I hire someone else to create a new spell?"

"No," it said again. "Your blood tie to Taika would interfere. But Noah can turn you."

Oh my God. "How?"

"He would have to shift into a full lion."

"Is he even capable of that after all these years?"

"It's still inside him. He just has to let it out."

"Then what? He would have to attack me?" She warded off a chill. "Lareina nearly killed him." Then there was the matter of the men she *had* killed. "Can you guarantee that I would survive?"

"No, but it isn't necessary for the exchange to be as brutal as what Lareina had done to him."

Jenny started. "What are you saying? That Noah could maul me in a gentler way and it could still work?"

"Only a minimal amount of blood has to be shed, so basically a few scratches would do. But he would have to resist the blind need to go further."

Lareina piped in from the sidelines. "And that wouldn't be easy. The need to be brutal would overpower him and so would the hunger for sex. They are side effects from the spell and Taika cautioned me beforehand about them. At the time I was certain that I would be able to control those urges. But once I was under the spell, I failed to fight it."

Jenny asked, "What happened after the spell was complete? How did you feel then?"

"The need to be brutal disappeared, and I felt remorse for

killing those men and for hurting Noah so badly. I don't regret my decision to spend eternity with my Sky Dweller, but if I could undo the damages I caused, I would."

Jenny's heart went tight. She wanted to spend the rest of her life with Noah, but there were frightening factors to consider.

"May I be released now?" Lareina asked. "Or do you have more questions?"

"You can go." As far as Jenny was concerned, there was no reason to keep her any longer.

Apparently the *sapiya* agreed. The women exchanged a quiet glance, then, *poof,* Lareina disappeared.

Jenny frowned at the vacant enclosure. Then she returned to the house and gave the *sapiya* blood from a steak. She didn't fix herself anything. She couldn't eat. All she could do was obsess about Noah.

"Do you think he would be able to resist the urge to be vicious?" she asked.

"Do you truly believe that he loves you?" came the reply.

"Yes. But he keeps saying that he doesn't."

"He does love you. He just hasn't admitted it to himself yet."

Did that mean he *could* resist? That he would be gentle with her? "You think it would turn out all right, don't you?"

"I cannot predict the outcome. All I know is that he loves you."

"If it happened, would I have the urge to turn someone else, and would I have to fight the brutality that comes with it?"

"No. Your connection to Taika would stop you from experiencing those side effects."

"How would the cats on my rescue react to me?"

"They would embrace the change. They accept shapeshifters as their own."

She thought about Valiente and Sandy. "Then why are the mountain lions leery around Noah?"

"His scent is awkward to them because he hasn't shifted all the way. They don't understand what he is."

But Jenny understood who and what he was, and although her "Beauty and the Beast" dream was gone, she was embarking on a new dream now.

She closed her eyes and envisioned herself as a shifter, a woman, a lion, moving between both worlds with the man she loved by her side.

She opened her eyes, wishing her grandfather was alive so she could talk to him about it. Would he support her dream? Would he embrace the idea of Jenny living forever and shifting into a cat?

Yes, she thought. He would. Grandpa would want her to follow her heart, to become what Noah was, as long as it was going to make her happy.

Grandpa knew what it was like to be alone, to lose almost everyone he'd loved. And if Jenny didn't do this, she would grow old and alone. She couldn't replace Noah. She would never love another man the way she loved him, and the only way to become his lifelong mate was for her to become a shifter.

While the *sapiya* finished soaking up the blood, Jenny called Noah and asked him to come over, praying he would listen to what she had to say.

Otherwise, what good was love if one of them was immortal and the other wasn't?

Fifteen

Noah couldn't believe his ears. He sat across from Jenny at a picnic bench at Big Cat Canyon, where she'd asked him to meet her and where she'd just spouted off her tale.

"You can't be serious," he said. "I would never—do you hear me?—*never* deliberately do to you what was done to me."

She argued her case. "The *sapiya* said that all it would take would be a few scratches. Just think of it as a gentle mauling."

"That's an oxymoron."

"I love you, Noah. And the *sapiya* says you love me, too."

"I'm sick of hearing about what that little stone told you. I'm not in love. I'm *fucking* not."

"Listen to the denial in your voice. Just listen to yourself. You sound like a child who's about to stomp his feet."

She was mocking him? Accusing him of throwing a temper tantrum? Ballsy chick. He could turn into his half-cat state and scratch the crap out of her just to teach her a lesson. Let alone how badly he could maul her if he went full-blown, as he was supposedly capable of doing.

"Get up," he said.

"What?"

"Get up and come with me." He went over to her side of the bench and grabbed her arm. "Now."

She tried to shrug away from him. "Stop it."

"Why? Is my grip too tight? Am I hurting you? Imagine that." He tugged a little harder. "I said come with me."

He practically dragged her along.

"Where are we going?" she asked.

"You'll see." He knew it wouldn't take long for her to become aware of where he was taking her. She obviously knew where every path on her property led. Still, he kept a tight hold on her.

Once she became aware, she said, "We're going to the mountain lions' enclosures? Why?"

To make a much-needed impact, he thought.

As soon as they approached the area, Valiente growled, but Noah figured the lion would start acting up. In fact, he'd counted on it.

"If you're trying to use them as a reason that I can't become a shapeshifter and still run this place, you're wrong," she said. "They would accept me just fine. They're leery of you because you haven't shifted all the way. Your presence wouldn't disturb them if your scent was more like theirs."

"I'm not trying to use them for that reason. And you're not telling me something that I don't already know."

"Then what's your point?"

He grabbed her shoulders and turned her directly toward Valiente. "Look at him. Look at the mood he's in." The lion stalked back and forth, its body taunt. "Would you purposely let him maul you? Would you trust him to give you just a few scratches?"

She went mum.

"Answer the question," he snapped.

"No, but he isn't you."

"That's a stupid answer. I would be just as dangerous as he is. Maybe more so because of the hunger that would overcome me. If Lareina couldn't keep herself in check, why would I be any different?"

"Because you love me."

"Quit saying that."

She persisted. "What about the connection we share? My ancestor is responsible for turning Lareina into a shapeshifter, and Lareina is responsible for turning you into one."

"That doesn't mean it's supposed to trickle down to you. Think about immortality, Jenny. Really think about it. You couldn't stay here forever. You'd have to move before people start to notice that you don't age. You'd have to change your identity, the way

I've been doing. And what about your family? What would you say to them?"

"Matt is my only family, and eventually I'd just have to tell him the truth. As for moving, I'd sell this place and start over as many times as I had to, opening new rescues. It doesn't matter, as long as I'm with you. Just say you'll do it, Noah."

Was there no reasoning with her? "What if I hurt you beyond repair? Or mauled you to death? I'm not agreeing to this madness."

"And I'm not giving up on becoming a shapeshifter. Maybe there's a way for Lareina to do it. Maybe there's a loophole in the spell the *sapiya* didn't tell me about."

That cinched it. Noah went ballistic. "Don't you let her get anywhere near you. Do you fucking hear me?"

"Stop shouting and stop cursing. Lareina doesn't have vicious urges anymore."

"Yeah, well, consider this—what if that so-called loophole backfired and she reverted back to what she was when she attacked me?" He shook her, hoping that he rattled her teeth, along with that hard head of hers. "I mean it—stay away from her." He raised his voice another octave. "If that bitch maimed or killed you, I'd want to die. And I *can't* die, so I'd be living the rest of my godforsaken life in misery."

"Why don't you just admit that you love me? Why else would you care so much?" She shoved her fists against his chest. "Just say it, Noah. Admit it."

Hell and damnation. He grabbed her wrists to hold her still. She was behaving like a little spitfire. "Knock it off."

"Say it!"

His emotions flew amok. Did he look like a clock with its hands spinning backward? With its springs coming loose? Whatever was happening to him, he wasn't about to acknowledge it as love. He would never give her that kind of leeway. "I'm not saying a damn thing. Nor am I going to attempt to turn you into what I am."

She blinked. Then her eyes went misty. "Please. If you don't turn me, our future is doomed."

She was begging him? That made it worse. "I can't take the chance."

"You'd be gentle. I know you would."

"But *I* don't know that I would, and that's more important than what you think you know."

She leaned against him, and he wrapped his arms around her. As the wind stirred lightly around them, they went silent in each other's embrace.

Finally, he stepped back. The moment was too soft and warm, and he couldn't bear the way being this close to her made him feel.

He said, "You should find yourself a mortal guy." He thought about the husband and children he'd assumed that she would have someday. "You should get married and have kids and grandkids and grow old like you're meant to."

"I'm meant to be with you."

"No, you're not. We should stop seeing each other. Now. Today. I can't do this anymore."

Her voice cracked. "You're ending it?"

"Yes." He was ending it. For good.

After Noah left, Jenny returned to the house, fighting tears. He'd walked away because he was concerned about hurting her. Wasn't that proof he wouldn't take the "mauling" further than it needed to go?

She didn't want to find herself a mortal guy. She wanted Noah, and if she couldn't convince him to turn her, then maybe there really was hope with Lareina.

She entered the kitchen, where she'd left the trinket box. She opened the lid, rousing the *sapiya*. She explained what had transpired between her and Noah, then asked if there was any way whatsoever that Lareina could turn her into a shapeshifter.

The answer was a resounding, "No."

"So, Noah is it? He's the only one who can do it?"

"Yes."

The tears she'd banked let loose, and she sat at the table, covered her face, and cried.

The *sapiya* rattled around in its box, drawing her attention. "Are you abandoning your quest?"

She uncovered her face. Was she?

No, she thought. Determined to stay strong, she grabbed a paper towel, dried her cheeks, and dabbed her runny nose.

Jenny spent the rest of the morning and a portion of the afternoon trying to figure out a course of action. She kept bouncing ideas around in her head.

Then it hit her.

She knew what she needed to do.

She said to the *sapiya*, "I'd like to see Lareina again. But I want you to bring her here, to my home. I want to talk to her without a barrier between us."

"Shall I do that now?"

"First I'm going to make some tea." Something to calm her nerves and something to offer Lareina. Funny thing, too. Less than a week ago Noah had made an offhand remark about Lareina not being the type to chat over afternoon tea. Hopefully Jenny was about to prove him wrong.

She brewed a soothing blend of mint and chamomile. She used her grandmother's floral-painted teapot and delicate china, including a cute little creamer and matching sugar bowl. She even opened a box of assorted cookies and arranged them on a plate.

After carrying everything into the living room and placing it on the coffee table, she waited in the hallway and told the *sapiya* she was ready for their guest.

Within a matter of minutes, Lareina appeared. She glanced

quickly around, puzzling, it appeared, over the vacant room and tea setup.

Jenny stepped forward and made herself known. "Would you care to join me?"

Lareina hesitated. "Earlier you put me in a cage and now you are entertaining me?"

"I didn't know if I could trust you earlier."

Lareina lifted her eyebrows. "And now you do?"

"You said that you were remorseful for what you did."

"I am."

"Then join me." Jenny gestured to the sofa.

The other woman took a seat and smoothed her dress. She was wearing the same filmy garment as before. Jenny sat beside her and poured the tea. Lareina added a bit of milk to her cup, and Jenny doctored hers with a spoonful of sugar.

How strangely civilized it was, sharing a refreshment with the shapeshifter who'd brutalized Noah. For a moment, Jenny questioned her own sanity.

Curious, she glanced at the *sapiya*. It sat silently in its box. It didn't seem concerned about her mental health. It obviously knew that she was making the right decision.

Jenny said to her guest, "I have a favor to ask of you."

After she explained, Lareina said, "Are you sure that Noah loves you?"

"I'm positive. Even my magic says so." But even more telling was the achingly tender way Noah had held her today. "Will you help me?"

The brunette nodded, and a bond was formed. That, too, was strangely civilized.

Once the details were finalized, Lareina reached for a cookie. "You look so much like Taika. She had the same soft quality, the same pale blond hair."

Jenny replied, "When Noah first mentioned you, he called you mysteriously beautiful. I can see how easily you seduced him. You could make any man want you."

"I didn't seduce the gods who captured me. They just took me."

"But then you found the man you loved. Tell me more about him. What's his name?"

"Cayo. He is strong and quiet, with eyes the color of the sky. All Sky Dwellers have blue eyes, even when they transform into lions."

"How did he feel about the spell that Taika cast? Was he worried about you desiring other men or harming them?"

"I convinced him that I wouldn't react that way. Later, he was devastated when he'd discovered what I'd done. It almost destroyed us. Sky Dwellers are not violent by nature, and he struggled to forgive me. But eventually he did."

"What do you think he'll say when you tell him that you're helping me become a shapeshifter?"

"He won't approve of your method, but he won't try to stop

me from getting involved. He'll understand the risk you're willing to take and how much Noah means to you."

"He means everything." And this was something she knew she had to do. To her, it wasn't a risk at all.

At six in the morning, Noah got a gut-wrenching phone call from Coyote.

The other man said, "Jenny discovered that Lareina can turn her. Something about a loophole in the spell. I was supposed to keep it a secret, but you know me. I just couldn't resist blabbing to you. Oh, and guess what? I get to be there when it happens. I'm so excited I can hardly stand it."

The wrenching worsened. "Do you realize how dangerous this is? Lareina could maim her for life. Or kill her. She could fucking die, and you're treating it like a spectator sport?"

"It's Jenny's choice."

"I'm not going to let her do this."

"You can't stop her. I'm leaving for the rescue now. It's going to be closed all day, but Jenny gave me a key to the main gate."

"Come and get me. I'm going with you."

"Jenny will be pissed if I do that."

"Since when do you care about pissing someone off? If you don't bring me with you, I'll follow you in my car and take the key away from you, even if I have to pound you into the ground to do it."

"Okay. Geez. I'll pick you up in front of the club. But I'm telling Jenny that you forced me into this."

Noah got out of bed and threw on a T-shirt and jeans. Soon he was riding shotgun in Coyote's luxury hybrid.

"Where on the rescue is it taking place?" Noah asked.

"In the empty enclosure where Lareina first appeared. Apparently Jenny and Lareina have struck up quite a friendship. Isn't that wild? The *sapiya* trusts Lareina, too."

Noah didn't. He knew what it was like to be her victim.

They arrived at the rescue in just less than an hour. Coyote unlocked the gate, and Noah took off in the direction of where the insanity was scheduled to take place.

"Wait up." Coyote sprinted behind him.

Noah increased his pace, leaving the out-of-shape shape-shifter in the dust.

When he saw Jenny alone in the cage, he rushed forward, intending to drag her out of it. The enclosure had two doors, with a secure area in between, designed to give caregivers a door between them and the animal inside. But Noah couldn't get through the first door, let alone gain entrance.

Both locks snapped magically into place, courtesy of the *sapiya*. The stone was hovering high in the air. If Noah could've caught it, he would have crushed it.

"What are you doing here?" Jenny asked, as he rattled the exterior door.

"Please don't do this." He gripped the metal. She looked soft and pretty, and oh, so fragile, like a dove that was about to be eaten by a lion.

"I have to," she responded.

Coyote finally showed up, huffing and puffing. "What did I miss?"

Neither of them answered him.

In the next god-awful moment, Lareina appeared.

Exactly as Noah remembered her.

Sixteen

Jenny saw the anguish in Noah's eyes. Clearly he believed the danger was real. Later, she would apologize for tricking him. But for now, this ruse was necessary.

Lareina didn't waste time. She shifted halfway, and with her feline features and the tawny streaks in her long dark hair, she looked similar to Noah when he was in that form. Jenny thought it made her wildly beautiful.

Her transformation continued, and once she was a full lion, she hissed at Noah, then turned and snarled at Jenny.

Pretending to be startled and frightened by Lareina's aggressiveness, Jenny gasped, then went perfectly still.

The two of them had rehearsed this scene, choreographing

every movement. With another growl, Lareina bunched her body, as if she intended to strike.

And strike hard.

Jenny screamed at the *sapiya*. "Take her away!"

Zip.

Lareina disappeared, and Jenny started to shake, feigning an adrenaline overload. Or partially feigning it. She *was* experiencing an adrenaline rush, hoping the rest of it went according to plan.

Luckily it did. As soon as the *sapiya* unlocked the enclosure, Noah came dashing in.

He drew her into his arms. "I told you not to trust her."

"I know. I know. You were right." She held on to him, taking a deep breath and preparing for the next phase.

Together, they headed for the double doors.

Click. Click. The *sapiya* relocked them.

For a moment, Noah seemed confused.

Jenny didn't say anything. She waited for him to make the connection and realize he'd been duped. It didn't take long.

His temper exploded. "There wasn't a loophole in the spell. You scammed me. You fucking scammed me. How could you do something like that?"

"I did it because I want to spend the rest of my life with you." She spoke in a tranquil tone, trying to keep him calm. "I'm sorry, but it was my only choice."

"*Your only choice?* You know I can't handle being locked up. Let me out of here. Now!"

She explained, as softly as she could. "Being locked up is going to help you shift all the way so you can turn me."

"According to who? You? The *sapiya?* That bitch Lareina? You're wrong. I already told you that I would never do it." He ignored her and slammed his gaze at Coyote. "I should have known it was bullshit since you were involved."

The other man responded, "Even if you'd suspected that it was a trick from the beginning, you still would have come here, just in case it was real."

"Yes, but I wouldn't have walked into this trap. This cage."

"I don't know about that," Coyote said. "I've heard that people in love do stupid things. But whatever the case, it'll be better for you if I'm not here. More sensual."

Noah narrowed his eyes. "What are you talking about?"

"Jenny is going to seduce you, nice and slow. That's the other little trick that's going to help you shift."

Noah shook his head. "No way. No frigging way."

Yes way, Jenny thought. After Coyote left, she moved closer to Noah.

"Don't touch me," he warned.

She didn't listen. She backed him into a corner and pressed her body against his. She kissed him, too, determined to make this happen.

. . .

Noah knew that he shouldn't return the kiss, but everything about her stirred temptation: the warmth of her mouth, the sweetly familiar scent of her skin, the flirty lines of her cotton summer dress.

She parted her lips, and their tongues met and mated. This wasn't right. She'd betrayed him. He should push her away. But he kept kissing her.

She toyed with his T-shirt, lifting it from the waistband of his jeans so she could run her fingers along his stomach. He sucked in his navel.

His cock was getting hard.

She put her hand against his fly and cupped the bulge. Smart girl. Stupid guy. How could he fall for her ploy?

She unzipped his pants. He needed to end it. *Now.* But he didn't.

While she stroked him, his breath rushed out. When she got down on her knees and freed him from his jeans, he prayed for someone to save him from the madness. She was going to give him a blow job inside the cage. Coyote was right. It was sensual as hell.

Jenny laved his cock, slowly, meticulously, as if his penis were her favorite flavor of ice cream.

Vanilla? Chocolate? Raspberry swirl?

Cripes, it felt good. She paid special attention to the head, rolling her tongue around. Then she went back to the shaft and licked out her name, letter by letter.

"I've wanted to do this to you ever since you did it to me," she said.

He shivered all the way to his toes.

She took him in her mouth, and he tunneled his hands through her hair. She pleasured him with sweet precision, but she didn't make him come.

She stood up, leaving him wanting more.

He watched her remove her clothes. She lowered the straps on her dress and slid the garment down.

Naked, she beckoned him to the ground. Noah couldn't seem to refuse. He stripped off his clothes and settled between her thighs.

Jenny put her arms around him, and he entered her, thrusting warm and deep. Her cunt contracted around his cock. They moved in unison.

The penetration got deeper, wetter, so damn perfect. Noah rocked back and forth, and she arched her hips.

"I want to be what you are," she said.

"No." He wouldn't let it go beyond sex. "I'm not going to turn you."

"But it only has to be a few scratches. A little blood."

Her words sounded hot, exciting. *A few scratches. A little blood.* Could it be that easy?

"No," he said again. *No. No. No.*

"Yes," she countered. "You're going to become a lion, a full lion, and you're going to skim your claws along my skin. Softly, and I'm going to moan when you do it."

Fuck, he thought. "Don't talk like that."

"I trust you."

"But you shouldn't. I have it in me to be brutal, Jenny. I've tied you to the bed. I've ripped a corset and petticoat off of your body. I've fucked you so hard, I've made you scream."

"But you never went too far, and you won't this time, either. Look how tenderly you're making love to me now."

That was true. He'd never had sex this gently before.

Jenny skimmed his jaw. "I love how it feels."

Noah's cock pulsed. His balls went unbelievably tight. He loved how it felt, too.

Desire. Full and thick.

Jenny made breathy sounds, and he captured her mouth in a kiss. She held on to him, pulling him closer.

Sweet synchronicity.

It didn't matter whose climax triggered whose. It simply happened at the same time. While she shuddered beneath him, he spilled into her, bathing her with his seed.

She didn't give him time to recuperate.

"Just a few scratches," she said again. "Just a little blood."

His brain short-circuited. She was gloriously bare, fresh from an orgasm, and ravenously alluring.

The intensity was too much to bear.

He shifted into half-lion form, but he felt the vicious urge to shift all the way, too. To tear into human flesh.

No!

He couldn't let himself become that kind of beast. He had to stop it.

Because the cage walls were closing in, he stood up, leaving Jenny on the ground. He started to pace, fighting the hunger.

He tried to call upon his tiger medicine to help him, to control the feeling. But it didn't help.

The craving roared through his veins.

"Get up," he told Jenny. "Stop being my prey."

She didn't budge. She remained on the dirt floor, offering herself to him like a sacrifice.

The scent from their lovemaking hung in the air. Romantic sex smelled the same as feral sex. His semen. Her juices. It made his appetite worse.

He snapped at the *sapiya*. "Get me the fuck out of here!"

The stone did nothing.

Noah was closer and closer to shifting.

Jenny reached out to him. Beckoning . . .

"Don't do this to me," he warned. "Don't make me want you again."

Too late. He did want her again. He wanted to put his mouth all over her. He got down on his hands and knees and ran his tongue along her flesh, filling himself with her mortal flavor.

She shivered at his touch, giving him permission to be primal.

His instincts betrayed him, and he lifted his head and growled, becoming what he'd been fighting.

A full-blown lion.

He could feel the reshaping and forming: his muscles growing stronger, his teeth getting sharper, his hands and feet turning into paws. It happened so quickly, he barely had time to separate his mind from the tawny pelt that covered his body.

God save Jenny, he thought. She lay beneath him, so quiet, so trusting. She would never make herself vulnerable to a wild animal, yet she was doing it with him.

How could she have that kind faith in him? He wanted to attack her, to slash and bite, to see her blood spill, to taste its liquid warmth.

Noah growled again. He was trapped within the cage. There was no way out. He couldn't run from the hunger.

He looked into her face. He could tell that her heart was pounding, but even so, she wasn't afraid. How could she not fear him? Didn't she know what he was thinking? How badly he wanted to rip into her?

If Lareina was beneath him, he would've already attacked her. He would've eaten her heart right out of her chest.

But it wasn't Lareina. It was Jenny. The woman he loved. *Yes, loved.*

He couldn't deny it any longer, and this was his chance to make her immortal, to be together forever. But could he scratch her softly? Could he control his urges?

Brave and beautiful, she reached up to stroke the side of his neck, reinforcing her trust in him.

Love. Faith. Togetherness.

While she petted him, he leaned into her touch and purred. If she trusted him that much, he could do it. He could be gentle. He knew he could. But where was the safest place to scratch her?

Not her breasts, not her stomach. Those areas were too sensitive. He zeroed in on her arm. The left one. She was still petting him with her right hand.

Noah bared his claws and lifted one paw in the air, reminding himself of how strong he was in this form. He had to be extremely careful.

Slowly, he swiped his claws down her skin. He heard her sharp intake of breath. No matter how gentle he was, he'd still cause her pain. He pulled back and saw lines of blood.

He'd done it. Oh, God, he'd done it.

He shifted back into human form, and she scooted quickly away from him. She was afraid now that it was over? Had he inflicted more damage than he'd realized? The cuts didn't look that deep, but how could he know for sure? Maybe he'd sliced her bone-deep.

"What's wrong?" he asked. "Oh, Jesus, Jenny. What did I do?"

"Don't worry. You did everything right. You just can't be around me right now."

"But I want to take you into the house and bandage your wounds, like I did when you hurt your knee."

"You can't help with the healing process. You can't tend to the person you're trying to turn. It's one of the rules of the spell."

He frowned. "What am I supposed to do? Leave you here by yourself?"

"I'm going to help her." Lareina appeared next to Jenny. The *sapiya* had brought her back.

"You?" He snapped at her.

She replied, "I'm sorry for what I did to you, Noah, but I promise I'll take good care of Jenny."

He didn't accept her apology, but he didn't argue with her, either. While he stayed silent, Lareina helped Jenny to her feet and aided her in getting dressed, or partially clothed, so as to not disturb her arm.

"I'll call Coyote and he'll come back for you," Jenny said.

He pulled on his jeans and yanked his shirt over his head. "How long do I have to wait to see you?"

"Until the transformation is complete. I'll get in touch with you when it happens."

She smiled at him, but it didn't ease his discomfort. He was leaving her with Lareina. It just seemed so twisted.

"I love you," he said to Jenny.

She smiled again. "I love you, too."

The *sapiya* unlocked the enclosure, and the women walked away with the little stone in tow. He watched them until they disappeared from view.

A moment later, he glanced down at his hands and noticed that he had Jenny's blood under his nails.

He was in for a long and grueling wait.

The day finally came. Jenny was so excited she couldn't sit still. Noah was on his way to her house.

She peered out the window, anxious to catch a glimpse of his vehicle as it entered her long, graveled driveway.

What would he be driving today? The Jaguar? The truck? Or another of his cars?

It was the truck, the big, red four-wheel drive.

She rushed onto the porch to greet him and smoothed her dress, the same one she'd worn the last time he'd seen her. The day he'd turned into a lion and scratched her. The day he'd told her that he loved her.

He parked the truck and got out. He was in human form, and so was Jenny. She descended the porch steps, and they gazed longingly at each other.

"I missed you," he said.

"I missed you, too." It had been only a few weeks, but the time had passed excruciatingly slowly. She extended her arm. "The marks are all gone."

He examined her unmarred skin. "How do you feel?"

"Wonderful." She smiled. "Immortal."

He smiled, too. Then he embraced her. Jenny couldn't have asked for a more thrilling reunion.

"Ready?" she asked.

He nodded, and they walked along her property, stopping at a secluded spot. She was anxious to show him how she'd changed.

She shifted halfway, giving him the opportunity to view her in that form. Because she'd been studying herself in the mirror since her transformation, she knew exactly what he was seeing. The tawny streaks in her hair were almost the same shade as her natural color, but the rest of her looked remarkably different. Her normally blue eyes were greenish gold and feline shaped. Every feature had a felid quality. She lifted her hands and extended her claws. She flashed her canine teeth, too.

"Damn. How gorgeous are you?"

"Being like one of my cats feels amazing."

"Are you naked under your dress?"

Her skin tingled. "Yes."

He shifted halfway, too. "Take it off."

Eager to please him, she lowered the garment and stepped out of it. She let him take a nice long look. Then, feeling deliciously feral, she trailed a claw down the front of his shirt and popped every single button.

He laughed and grabbed her, pushing her against a tree. They kissed deep and rough, like the shapeshifters they were.

"Turn around," he said.

She did his bidding and planted her hands on the bark. He

shoved his jeans down and thrust full hilt inside her. While he pumped his hips, while he fucked her good and hard, she scratched the wood. She even carved a big jagged heart into it.

He snarled lustfully against her ear. "This is going to happen fast."

Fast worked for her. She pushed back against his thrusts, making it even more savage.

Noah pressed a hand against the front of her pussy, rubbing back and forth. He detonated her clit, and she went off like a bomb, sparks shooting from her core.

One orgasm down. More to follow.

He made her come, too many times to count. She loved being a she-cat. This was her destiny, the untamed creature she was meant to be.

Noah scraped the back of her neck with his canines. It didn't matter how animalistic he got; she could take it.

She could dish it out, too.

She screamed like a banshee, like a female lion, all sexed up. That made her mate come. He trembled, shuddered, and released a fierce growl. Rife with carnal need, he thrust one last time, and his semen shot out.

Jenny caught her breath and closed her eyes. Sublime pleasure. Noah held her quietly.

A short time later, she put her dress back on, and he righted his pants. They sat under the tree, both of them still in half-cat form.

"Have you shifted all the way yet?" he asked her.

She nodded. "It was the most freeing feeling. Have you done it since you turned me?"

"No. But I've been cooped up in the city. Maybe we can do it together tonight?"

She smiled. "Absolutely." Mountain lions were wonderfully nocturnal, and now Jenny was, too. She gestured to the hills on her land. "We can enjoy our own private sanctuary." She glanced in the direction of the house. "Are you going to move in with me?"

"Damn straight, I am. I'm going to keep the club, too, but I'll hire someone else to manage it. Maybe one of the vampires."

"Are you ever going to forgive Lareina?"

"Deep down, I think I already have. Without her, Coyote, and the *sapiya*, you couldn't have tricked me and we wouldn't be together like this." He stretched out his legs. "That reminds me—what are you going to do about the *sapiya*? Are you keeping the stone or are you going to set it free?"

"I'll do whatever it wants me to do."

"It'll probably choose to remain with you." He spoke reverently. "Who wouldn't want to be with you forever?"

She leaned forward and kissed him, and as the kiss intensified, so did their instincts, their hunger.

They tumbled in the grass, anxious to make love again. And this was how it was going to be for the rest of their lives, she thought.

Hot. Thrilling. Dangerously meaningful.

They'd created a new fairy tale, a new kind of eternity.

"Beast and the Beast." Wild ever after.